Hey Mina

Wolf Pack

EDO VAN BELKOM

Tundra Books

To Lilian, Vivian, and Lynda.

Published in Canada by Tundra Books,
481 University Avenue, Toronto, Ontario M5G 2E9

Published in the United States by Tundra Books of Northern New York,
P.O. Box 1030, Plattsburgh, New York 12901

Library of Congress Control Number: 2004102053

National Library of Canada Cataloguing in Publication

van Belkom, Edo
    Wolf pack / Edo van Belkom.

ISBN 0-88776-669-2

    I. Title.

PS8593.A53753W64 2004   JC813'.54   C2004-900841-2

We acknowledge the financial support of the Government of Canada
through the Book Publishing Industry Development Program (BPIDP)
and that of the Government of Ontario through the Ontario Media
Development Corporation's Ontario Book Initiative. We further
acknowledge the support of the Canada Council for the Arts and the
Ontario Arts Council for our publishing program.

Design: Cindy Elisabeth Reichle

Printed and bound in Canada

This book is printed on acid-free paper that is
100% ancient-forest friendly (40% post-consumer recycled).

1 2 3 4 5 6   09 08 07 06 05 04

Prologue

Garrett Brock had been fighting the fire for days, but this was the closest he'd come to the flames. They were less than fifty yards away now, ribbons of fire creeping toward him through the undergrowth. Every so often, the flames would overtake some small tree or patch of dry brush, and there would be an explosion, sending sparks flying into the air and a new wall of flame racing through the forest.

Garrett was a member of a four-man crew sent in to dig a firebreak in the hopes of containing the fire on the west side of Redstone. If the firebreak failed, the town would have to be evacuated and the purpose of the firefight would shift from controlling the fire to saving the town.

A sudden gust of wind blew a heavy cloud of ash and smoke eastward. The smoke washed over Garrett in a wave, clogging his lungs and forcing him to double over and cough to clear his throat. When he looked up again, the other members of his crew were gone from sight, shrouded in the pall of thick gray smoke.

The fire kept coming. He could feel its heat pressing against his body and wanted to run. But he steeled himself against the urge and kept working to widen the break.

As he thrust his shovel into the ground, he caught sight of something out of the corner of his eye. There was movement of some kind, coming toward him from the direction of the fire.

He stood up and looked west. His first thought was that one of his fellow crew members had been trapped by the flames, but that wasn't it. The thing was moving too fast. It appeared out of the smoke and flames like a gray ghost, bounding toward him as if running for its life.

Garrett knew he should move, that he should get out of its way, but it was approaching rapidly. What's more, he was transfixed by the sight of it, a big silver-gray wolf bounding toward him with an open maw. Four . . . five strides and it was upon him.

He dropped his shovel and put up his hands to protect himself, but the animal charged right past him, knocking him onto his back and sending his hard hat spinning across the forest floor.

When he recovered his bearings, Garrett sat up and looked behind him. The wolf seemed to be sniffing around inside a small hollow on the other side of the firebreak. A moment later it was running back toward him, streaking past the spot where he still lay on the ground, and heading straight for the fire. Back into the flames.

The wind picked up, pushing ever eastward. The fire grew in intensity, whole trees igniting like match heads, and the animal had gone back into the heart of it.

Garrett got to his feet, picked up his shovel, put his hard hat on his head, and got back to work on the firebreak. But after he'd moved just a few shovelfuls of earth, the wolf reappeared. Patches of its fur were on fire, streaming smoke behind it as it ran. Its maw was open again, but this time Garrett noticed there was something small and black inside it.

He remained on his feet, watching the wolf run past him. It returned to the hollow on the other side of the break and began sniffing around with its snout, as if it were digging a hole or maybe burying something with its muzzle.

And then it stood up on all fours, looking back at the fire.

Garrett felt a needle of dread pierce his heart. "No," he said under his breath. "Don't do it!"

Once again, the wolf headed back toward the fire, this time slowing as it passed him and turning its head in Garrett's direction as if it had heard him speak. For a moment their eyes made contact. There was fear in the wolf's eyes, and desperation too, perhaps even a plea for help.

Garrett didn't know what to do, but he had to try something. "Stop!" he shouted, waving his arms in a futile attempt to command the animal.

But the wolf was already on the move, charging back into the forest and disappearing behind the wall of flame.

Garrett watched the fire, anxiously waiting for the wolf to reappear. But it never did.

Minutes later the wind picked up again – and turned. It was blowing westward now, doubling the fire back onto itself. For a short time the flames rose higher, burning hotter than they had in days.

But in just a few hours, the fire had all but burnt itself out.

Then it began to rain.

•◆•

It was a short walk out of the bush to the road. But instead of heading for the road, Garrett Brock took a slight detour, returning to the spot where he'd seen the wolf.

The wolf itself was surely dead. Several of the other rangers had mentioned coming across a few large carcasses, and many smaller ones, among the ashes. But Garrett wasn't looking for the wolf. What he wanted to know was what the wolf had carried out of the fire and deposited in the hollow on the other side of the firebreak.

When he found the break, he began walking along it as if along a trail. Much of the forest on the west side of the firebreak was still smoldering, silently smoking under the fall of rain. In contrast, the east side, the side with the hollow, was still green and lush, although much of the forest's luster had been dulled by soot and falling ash.

Garrett stopped to check his bearings. The west side of the break was unrecognizable, having been awash with flame the last time he'd seen it. The east side was familiar to him, though, and he knew he was close to the spot where he'd seen the wolf. He set his feet and searched the forest for the hollow. It took him less than a minute to find it, slightly farther along the break than he remembered, but unmistakable once he'd found it.

He moved toward the hollow slowly, not sure what he might find there. As he neared, he began stepping cautiously over the forest floor, careful not to step on any branches that could snap or make a loud or sudden noise.

And then he heard it – a series of low growling sounds.

He stopped in his tracks a moment, unsure whether to move closer or back away.

The growling sounds continued, but now there were several yelps that had been added to the mix.

He stepped forward again, moving into a position where he could peer over a fallen log and down into the hollow.

"Oh my God!" he gasped.

There, nestled into the tight confines of the hollow, were four tiny wolf cubs, each one climbing over the other in an attempt to find a more comfortable position. Or perhaps they were hungry and searching blindly for their mother.

If that was the case, they'd be searching for a long, long time. That is, if a predator didn't happen by and eat them first.

Garrett had no choice but to take the cubs with him. He slipped off his pack, took off his jacket, and laid it out on the forest floor. Then he slid down into the hollow and picked up the cubs, one at a time, and set them onto his jacket. When they were all nestled comfortably, he wrapped up the cubs and tied off the sleeves, turning the jacket into a sack. There were still growls coming from the cubs, but those were slowly becoming fainter as the animals realized they were now warm and out of the rain, and soon they'd be fed.

Garrett slipped on his backpack and – carrying his wolf-filled jacket in his right hand – headed back toward the firebreak and out of the forest.

•–•

Garrett's wife, Phyllis, was waiting at the front door to greet him.

The Brocks lived in a modest house just off the main highway outside Redstone. Although not a ranger herself, Phyllis worked for the Forest Service as well and often helped Garrett man the watchtowers during fire season, as well as educate school children about forest conservation during the winter months.

"I heard the fire was under control," she said. "They said on the radio it looked like it was going to head straight into Redstone, but then it just –"

"Burned itself out, I know," Garrett said.

Phyllis looked at him for a moment, her eyes narrowing slightly. "You were in trouble, weren't you?"

"For a little while there, yeah."

She put her arms around him and gave him a long, tight hug.

Garrett returned the embrace with his left arm, but didn't let go of the bundled jacket still clenched in his right hand.

"What's in the bag?" she said, noticing his extended arm.

He hesitated, then said, "I couldn't leave them."

"Another animal?" she said, a hint of disappointment in her voice. "I still haven't replaced the curtains from when you brought home that bobcat last year."

Garrett ignored her, knowing that she couldn't possibly protest after she saw them. He knelt down, placed his jacket on the floor, and began to carefully untie the arms. "They would have died if I'd left them in the forest."

Phyllis looked unconvinced.

But then he opened up the jacket to reveal the four wolf cubs huddled together in a tight mass of gray-white fur.

Phyllis raised a hand to her mouth.

"Well?"

"They must be hungry," she said, already on her way to the kitchen to warm up some milk.

◆◆◆

After fighting the fire for several days, Garrett slept like a fallen log.

Phyllis, on the other hand, couldn't sleep a wink. After feeding the cubs, then preparing a box for them in the garage, she had stayed up past midnight just watching the animals sleep. They'd looked so tiny and frail that it was a wonder they'd survived the fire at all.

Were there only four cubs in the litter? she wondered. Garrett had said that the mother had gone back into the fire, most likely to retrieve another cub. But whether there had been another cub, or even two, these four had survived, and she and Garrett would do everything they could to make sure they grew up strong and healthy so they could be reintroduced to the forest when the time came.

Phyllis glanced at the clock on the nightstand. It was just after three in the morning, and the cubs might be hungry. Even if they weren't, it wouldn't hurt to look in on them again.

She threw back the covers and slid off the bed without disturbing Garrett. Then she put on her slippers, wrapped herself in a housecoat, and headed to the garage to sneak a peek at the cubs.

She'd left the door leading into the garage from the house open so heat from inside the house would keep the garage warm. Still, Phyllis noticed a drop in temperature when she stepped from the house into the garage. She made a mental note to buy an electric space heater in the morning.

There was no sound coming from the box, and Phyllis guessed the cubs were also sleeping soundly after their harrowing ordeal. Not wanting to disturb them, she crept silently up to the box and peered over the side.

Her eyes suddenly went wide. And she gasped.

"Garrett!" she cried.

No answer.

"Garrett, come here!" she screamed.

"What?" came the faint response from the bedroom.

"Come here! Come and see!"

Footsteps inside the house and a knock on the wall as Garrett tried to get to the garage as fast as he could.

"What is it?" he said, finally stumbling through the doorway into the garage.

"Look!" said Phyllis, pointing down into the box.

Garrett shuffled across the garage floor, wiped the sleep from his eyes, and looked.

"Holy . . ." his voice trailed off in disbelief.

In the box were four human infants.

Fifteen Years Later

Chapter 1

"Okay, how about this?" Noble said. He rolled up his sleeve and raised his right arm over his head. Then he closed his eyes and chewed his bottom lip. After several moments . . . hair began to appear on his arm.

"All right!" said Argus, clapping his hands together in approval.

Noble continued the partial transformation, opening and closing his hand until the arm, from elbow to fingertip, was covered by a thick mat of gray hair. Then he clenched his hand in a tight fist and held it closed as his forearm muscles writhed and rippled under the skin. The arm was unnaturally large now, like that of a bodybuilder on the body of an otherwise normal fifteen-year-old boy.

"You must have been practicing," said Tora, the lone female of the group. She was a beautiful young woman, with long brown locks that were naturally highlighted by a streak of golden blond that ran right through the middle of her hair like a ray of sunshine.

"You bet I have," Noble smiled. "It beats doing homework."

The others laughed in agreement.

Noble was the unofficial leader of the pack. Although they were all the same age, he seemed older and wiser than his brothers and sister and was the one the others always turned to for help. He was also handsome, not just good looking, but teen-idol cute. He'd also begun shaving on a daily basis, which made him even more desirable to the girls at school.

"Let me try," said Argus, rolling up his own shirt sleeve.

Argus was the largest of the three males in the pack. Although he easily had the strength to challenge Noble for the position of Alpha Male, he knew that Noble's mind was better suited for the role of leadership – especially for their life among humans. Argus preferred fighting over thinking, but understood that not all problems could be solved by way of the claw. He had rugged good looks, but his features weren't as refined as Noble's. Most striking of all were his eyes, one of which was green, the other blue. He'd been teased about his eyes as a child, but these days no one would dare, since it was a sure way to provoke Argus into a fight, which was something that he had yet to lose.

Argus made a fist and the hair began to sprout along the top side of his arm.

"Hey, I'm doing it," he said, pulling his sleeve farther up his arm and flexing his bicep.

Suddenly, the entire arm changed into its werewolf form, something halfway between human and wolf. The increased muscle mass in the arm first stretched then tore Argus's sleeve.

Harlan, the third male, laughed. "Phyllis is going to kill you when we get home."

Argus sneered at him. "Not if I tell her it's your fault." He gave Harlan a push with his oversized arm, and the smaller boy stumbled backward, then fell onto the forest floor.

But instead of landing heavily on the humus, Harlan tucked his body into a tight ball, rolled, and wound up in a standing position, his legs bent, his teeth clenched, and his lips pulled back in a snarl.

Harlan was the runt of the litter and could best be described as bony, no matter what form he was in. He still hadn't matured like the others had, but he was hopeful that puberty would be the great equalizer among them. Although he could easily handle himself against humans in his wolf form, he was always dwarfed by the lupine versions of Noble, Argus, and even Tora.

"Relax Harlan," Noble commanded. "He was just kidding around."

Harlan remained poised and ready for a fight.

"Weren't you, Argus?"

Argus looked at Noble, then turned to face Harlan. "Yeah, I didn't mean to push you so hard. Sorry."

Harlan relaxed slightly and smiled. Then he raised his right arm, pulled back the sleeve of his sweatshirt, and said, "That's okay, big man. It's not your fault you can't control something as basic as shape shifting."

Harlan's arm was perfectly transformed with well-defined musculature, thick silver-gray hair, and a set of claws that were as sharp as razors.

Argus didn't appreciate being shown up, especially by Harlan. He was about to put his little brother in his place when Tora jumped between them in full wolf form.

Harlan and Argus stepped back.

Noble looked at Tora, admiring the yellow-white streak that ran back from her head and down between her shoulder blades. "It looks like someone wants to go for a run."

Tora bounded away, then stopped at the edge of the clearing, waiting for the rest of them to join her.

"Well?" Noble asked the others.

"Sure," said Harlan.

"A run would be good," Argus agreed.

In moments the boys had transformed into three silver-gray wolves, Harlan being the smallest, Argus the largest.

The middle-sized wolf ran toward the trees, stopping next to Tora, and gestured for her to take the lead.

Without another sound, the lone female bounded into the forest, her three brothers following close behind.

•◦•

"All right," said Doctor Edward Monk. "Let me know when you're ready."

The cameraman, a stocky dark-haired man in his twenties named Bruno, adjusted the camera on his shoulder. The soundman, a slightly built man in his fifties named Charles, put a finger to his ear and adjusted the levels on the recorder that hung from his shoulder and rode on his right hip like a saddle bag.

A few seconds later Charles nodded.

"Speed," said Bruno.

"For more than a hundred years, environmentalists have looked upon fire as the enemy," the doctor began, stepping lightly through the forest along a route he'd mapped out and rehearsed several times before. "But in recent years, Mother Nature has been telling us a vastly different story."

Charles and Bruno matched the doctor's progress step-for-step.

"Fire has been a natural part of forest and grassland ecosystems since there have been trees and grass to burn." Doctor Monk winced at the line, then said, "Cut!"

"What's wrong?" asked Bruno.

"That didn't sound right," said Monk.

Charles slipped off his headphones. "Sounded fine to me."

"No, I mean the words didn't sound right. Not clever enough."

Charles rolled his eyes.

"Those were the words you scripted," Bruno offered.

17

"But they read better than they sounded."

Bruno gave a little shrug. "Whatever."

"Okay, I'll do the last line again," Monk said. "But take a different angle so we can cut it any way we want to."

Bruno took a look around, moved several paces to his right, then said, "Speed."

"Fire has been a natural part of forest and grassland ecosystems since there have been trees and grass on God's green Earth." That sounded even worse, but the doctor continued. "In fact, ecosystems depend on fire for renewal. After a burn, many forms of life survive, and the mineral-rich ash that's left behind is perfect for re-invigorating the soil with nutrients, which in turn gives the regeneration process a kick-start by creating ideal growing conditions."

The doctor turned along his route so that a slight clearing could be seen over his left shoulder. "Fires also create clearings that allow sunlight to penetrate to the forest floor, giving different kinds of vegetation the chance to grow. This helps give the forest some variety between old and new growth, and a larger variety of habitats supporting different species of insects, mammals, and birds."

Bruno began to pan away from the doctor to get a wide shot of the new forest.

"In short, fire renews and recycles the forest, and is an important part of an ecosystem's life cycle, as evidenced by this section of Redstone Forest, an area that was ravaged by fire fifteen years ago but is now teeming with new growth and new life forms."

The doctor remained still, giving Bruno time to get a

nice panorama of the forest that they would dissolve into a shot of the trees as it looked immediately following the fire.

After about ten seconds, the doctor said, "Cut!"

But Bruno kept filming.

"I said, *cut!*"

Bruno waved at the doctor to be quiet, then pointed in the direction he was shooting.

The doctor squinted at first, not sure what he was seeing. But then he said, "Oh my God!"

In the distance, four kids, almost adults really, were stripping out of their clothes, and then – it was almost too incredible to believe – began transforming themselves into wolves.

When they were all – Doctor Monk still couldn't believe it – *changed*, they bounded off into the forest together, as if they were all members of the same pack.

"Please," the doctor said. "Please tell me that you got all of that on tape."

Bruno cracked a smile and nodded. "Zoomed in on them pretty good. I got a close up of one of them changing, almost full frame."

"Give me the tape!" Monk demanded.

"There's still twenty minutes left on it."

"I don't care, give it to me!"

"But what if they come back?"

"Then put in a new tape, and give that one to me!"

Bruno sighed, then lifted the camera off his shoulder, popped the tape out of the side of the machine, and handed it over to Doctor Monk.

The doctor snatched the tape away.

"You're welcome," Bruno said under his breath as he tore the plastic wrap off a brand new tape and slid it into his machine.

Monk studied the tape closely, turning it over slowly in his hands. After several moments, he looked up and said, "David Suzuki never got footage like this."

•—•—•

The four wolves returned to the clearing about a half-hour later, tongues lolling from the sides of their mouths in evidence of a long, hard run.

The transformation back into human form took no time at all, and in minutes they were all but dressed in their clothes.

"Phyllis is going to kill me," Argus said, examining the tear he'd put in his shirt sleeve.

"No she won't," said Noble. "She'll understand."

Tora took a look at the tear. "She might even repair it and hand the shirt down to Harlan."

Argus laughed at that, but Harlan didn't even crack a smile.

"Quiet!" Noble said, throwing up his right hand.

"What is it?" asked Tora.

"I heard something," he said. "Over there."

The four of them all looked in the direction Noble was pointing.

Harlan shrugged. "I don't see anything."

Noble started walking without another word.

The others followed.

He'd gone thirty or forty paces before stopping at the opposite end of the clearing.

Argus came up behind Noble and said, "What's wrong?"

"Someone was here," Noble said, pointing to parts of the forest floor that had been flattened by footprints. "Two, maybe three people."

Tora looked about the forest. "Who were they?"

Noble shook his head. "Don't know."

"Maybe they were hikers," suggested Harlan.

Noble considered that for a while, then said, "Yeah, maybe they were hikers."

But as the four of them turned to head home, Noble had a bad feeling that the people who'd been here were not hikers. Hikers moved in-line along a trail. These people had stood around in one place for a long time. But if they weren't hikers, what were they doing this deep in the forest?

Chapter 2

The Brock home was nestled into a small valley on the leeward side of the Nechako Range of mountains in central British Columbia. It was a four-bedroom stone building with a large steel storage shed out back and a 100-foot tower farther up the mountain slope. Garrett Brock had taken over the house and the grounds when he'd been put in charge of the forest around Redstone. That had been more than ten years ago. Since that time, several improvements had been made to the house in order to make it more accommodating to Garrett's wife, Phyllis, and his four adopted children.

"There's a fire on the hearth," said Noble as he stopped on the crest of a ridge about a quarter mile from the house.

Harlan sniffed at the air. "Not only that," he said, "but it smells like it's hamburgers for supper."

Argus sniffed the air himself. "I don't smell anything."

"You want to bet on it?" Harlan challenged Argus.

"Not a bet I'd like to take," said Tora.

Despite his lack of size, or perhaps because of it, Harlan had developed the keenest sense of smell of the four of them. It wasn't like he'd never made a mistake, but when he detected and identified a scent, he was rarely proven wrong.

Argus ignored Harlan's words and bounded down the path. "Then we've got even more reason to hurry home."

When they arrived home, Ranger Brock was out on the large wooden deck behind the house talking to Phyllis.

"Smells good," Argus said, coming around to look at the burgers sizzling on the gas grill.

"Told you," said Harlan.

"Did anyone call?" Tora asked.

"Were you expecting a call?" Phyllis asked.

Harlan giggled. "When she asks if anyone called, what she's really asking is if Michael Martin called."

Michael Martin was a classmate and son of Sergeant Martin, the officer in charge of the Redstone detachment of the Royal Canadian Mounted Police. Of all the boys at school, Michael was the only one who wasn't afraid of her brothers and didn't seem to mind Tora's mood swings and bad hair days – which, truth be told, could sometimes be really bad.

"Michael Martin?" said Ranger Brock, a touch of surprise in his voice. "I didn't know you were sweet on him."

"I'm not," Tora said quickly.

Argus laughed. "Not much."

"I'm not," she repeated, this time with a swing of her long flowing hair. "He's sweet on me."

"I see," said Phyllis. "Well, there have been no calls for any of you, from Michael Martin or anyone else for that matter."

The four of them turned to head into the house when Phyllis caught sight of Argus's shirt. "What happened here?" she asked, tugging on his torn sleeve.

"Harlan –" Argus began, but stopped himself.

"Harlan what?"

"Harlan smelled the hamburgers cooking and I started running through the forest."

"And?"

Argus looked over at Noble. "I guess I must've caught my shirt on a branch."

Noble smiled approvingly, giving Argus a slight nod.

Phyllis sighed and took a closer look at the shirt. "I guess I could fix it . . . or make it into a short-sleeve shirt for Harlan."

Now it was Argus's turn to smile.

Harlan shook his head, and Tora gave him a playful slap on the shoulder.

"Put it in the wash," said Phyllis, "then get ready for supper."

Argus, Tora, and Harlan headed inside. Noble remained on the deck with Garrett and Phyllis.

"What is it?" the ranger asked. He had raised the pack

since they were cubs and he could always tell when something was on their minds – like now.

"Is there anything going on in the forest right now?" Noble asked.

"What do you mean?"

Noble hesitated, unsure how to phrase the question. "Is there anything going on in the forest right now that's . . . well, out of the ordinary?"

"Why? What did you see?"

Noble shrugged. "Nothing really. Just some tracks, but not the kind left by hikers. These were spread out, like people had been standing around in one place for a long time."

Ranger Brock crossed his arms and looked at the mountains behind the house. He often did that when he was thinking, as if just the sight of the majestic rises and snow-capped peaks helped him think more clearly. "There's a crew in the area doing a piece on the forest for the Discovery Channel," he said. "I think it's being led by Doctor Edward Monk."

"The geneticist?"

"Yeah. He's doing a piece about growth and regeneration after a fire. He picked Redstone because . . . well . . ."

"Then it must have been him and his crew."

"Did you see them?"

Noble shook his head. "Just their tracks."

"I'll have to keep an eye out for him, then," the ranger said. "I hear the doctor's quite a character."

•–•

"Rewind it!" said Doctor Monk. "I want to see it again!"

Bruno let out a sigh. "But we've already seen it twelve times."

"I don't care if we've seen it a hundred times," Monk said. "Let me see it again."

Bruno emptied the last of his Diet Coke in a gulp, tossed the can into the garbage, and rewound the tape inside the camera for the doctor.

After taping the kids in the forest, Monk and his crew had retreated to their room at the Redstone Inn to examine the footage in private. Bruno had hooked up his camera to a monitor so they all could see what he had taped.

The first time through, each one of them had been left speechless. In fact they watched it four times before anyone said a word.

"Incredible," Monk said.

"Fascinating," Charles muttered.

"Wow!" was all Bruno could come up with.

After they'd watched it four more times, Charles lay back on one of the beds, threatening to drift off to sleep. Bruno might have done the same if Monk hadn't needed him to operate the camera.

The camera clicked, signaling that the tape was fully rewound. "Here you go," he said, and pressed *play*.

On the black and white monitor was a shot of Doctor Monk preparing himself for his introduction. Bruno fast-forwarded through that part until the doctor was slowly sliding to the right of the screen and out of the frame.

Bruno slowed the tape to normal speed, and things suddenly became clearer.

In the distance, there were four young adults, laughing and joking as if they might be hanging out on a street corner after school. The four of them slowly grew larger on the screen until they filled it entirely. One of the boys' arms suddenly bulked up, changing shape as it did until it was rippling with muscle and covered by a thick mat of hair.

"Amazing," Monk whispered, even after seeing the footage a dozen times.

Then the screen became filled by the smallest of the group as he shed his clothes and miraculously transformed from a human being into a wolf.

A WOLF.

Then the camera pulled back slightly so that now there were four wolves on the screen where moments before there had been four human teenagers.

"Absolutely amazing," the doctor said.

"Yes it is," Bruno said. "Now can I shut this off and get to sleep."

"Do you have any idea what this footage means?" Monk said, ignoring Bruno's request.

Bruno began packing up his camera, deciding not to wait for the doctor's approval. "Prime-time television special, at least," he said. "I've seen whole hours of television built up around less."

Charles cleared his throat and said, "The lecture circuit could be pretty profitable. I've heard of some speakers earning ten and twenty thousand dollars a night. With the right sort of talk and this footage, you could probably charge fifty thousand a night, easy."

Monk laughed at both of them and shook his head slightly. "You two are thinking too small," he said. "This videotape is unlike anything anyone's ever seen before, but . . ."

He paused and for a moment it seemed as if he wasn't going to finish his thought.

"But what?" prodded Charles.

"But . . . it's only the beginning."

Charles and Bruno glanced at each other, confused looks on their faces.

"I'm going to capture one of those creatures," Monk said, a fire alight in his eyes. "Alive!"

Chapter 3

The next day at school was like most others for the pack, full of problems that few at Redstone Secondary School could even begin to imagine. While most of the human teenagers at the school were dealing with raging hormones and acne, the four members of the pack had all that to worry about, and more. Much more.

During lunch period, Noble spotted Tora sitting alone at a table in the far corner of the cafeteria. Her back was to him and to the rest of the students, and her head seemed to be slumped forward, as if she were trying to hide herself from view.

Noble pulled up a chair next to her. "How's it going?" he said.

Tora bit into a pepperette and tore the meat stick apart with a hard jerk of her hand. "Lousy."

"Why? What happened?" Noble asked, keeping his voice even.

Tora turned her head away for a moment, as if holding back a tear, then lifted her head to look back across the table at Noble. "I was changing for gym class this morning, and when I took off my jeans my legs were covered in hair."

Noble pressed his lips together to keep himself from making some wisecrack he might later regret.

"Below my knees, and even my thighs. And it wasn't just a little fuzz, either. It was hair. Thick, black hair!"

Noble was at a loss for what to say. Even though they were werewolves, that didn't stop them from going through puberty like the rest of their classmates. And *because* they were werewolves, all kinds of strange things could happen, usually at the worst possible time. Noble once had a similar experience with his eyebrows growing together overnight while he slept, but he'd been able to fix the problem easily enough in the morning with a pair of tweezers and a razor before heading off to school. Obviously, Tora hadn't been so lucky. Still, he had to say *something* to try to comfort her.

"I'm sure it wasn't that bad –"

"No, it was that bad!" she said, pounding a fist onto the table. "It was terrible. Maria Abruzzo called me a dog . . . a hairy dog."

Noble smiled at that. "Yeah, well, Maria Abruzzo is one to talk with that mustache of hers."

The corners of Tora's mouth turned up in a hint of a smile. "You noticed it too?"

"'Course I did," Noble said. "I mean, you're a lycanthrope, but what's her excuse?"

Tora smiled and let out a little laugh. "That's right."

Noble dropped his lunch on the table just as Argus showed up to join them. He wasn't saying anything, but from the way his nose was twitching, it was obvious he was in a foul mood.

"What? Not you too?"

Argus sat down and dropped his books onto the empty seat by his side. "Coach Quinn asked me to join the football team. Again!"

"What'd you tell him?"

"I told him no. Again!"

Noble nodded. With his size, Argus was an obvious candidate for lineman on the Redstone Warriors senior football team, but the pack had decided long ago – in consultation with Ranger Brock – that playing football on a team of humans would be unfair to the other players. Even if the pack promised not to use their shape shifting abilities to play the game, the temptation would always be there for them to change their form slightly to score a winning touchdown or hurt an opposing player. Coach Quinn didn't bother Noble or Harlan about playing on the team, but Argus's size made him the man's favorite target. For some reason, the coach felt he could win a provincial championship if only Argus centered the offensive line.

"He pressed me this time, questioning my loyalty to the school. And then he said, if I didn't want to play football there were a few skirts that needed filling on the cheer-leading squad."

Noble let a faint whistle escape his lips, fearing the worst. "And you told him . . ."

"I said, 'And I bet one of them is just your size.'"

"Whoa!" Tora said.

Noble let out a sigh, shook his head twice, and raised his right hand for a high-five. "Good answer."

"Yeah, but what he said still gets under my skin."

"I can see that," Noble said, noticing that Argus seemed a bit bigger than usual, as if all his pent-up rage was roiling just under the surface, eager for a release.

At that moment, there was laughter at the far end of the cafeteria. Harlan had just entered and people were giggling and laughing as he passed them.

"What now?" Noble wanted to know.

Harlan hurried across the room, looking at everyone around him as if trying to see what was so damn funny?

"Turn around," Noble said, when he reached their table.

Harlan turned around.

Taped to his back was a small piece of paper with words printed in thick black ink:

I'M A DuFUs.

Noble reached up and pulled the paper off Harlan's back.

"What was it?"

Noble shook his head. "Nothing."

Harlan didn't believe him. "No, c'mon, what was it?"

Tora grabbed Harlan by the arm and pulled him down onto the seat next to her. "He already told you. It was nothing."

Harlan made himself comfortable, and, for the next few moments, not one of them said a word.

Finally Noble said, "I think we need to go for another run tonight."

"Yes!" Argus nodded.

"A real long run through the forest."

"I'm so there," said Harlan.

"That's a good idea," Tora said. "A really good idea."

• ◆ •

"That's *it*?" said Charles the soundman as he stood over the large hole in the ground that Bruno had spent most of the day digging.

"Oldest trick in the book," said Bruno, readying his camera in preparation for the shoot. Doctor Monk had asked them to tape a short segment of him in front of the trap, just in case they needed the footage for the television special Monk was building around the images they'd recorded the previous day.

"Yes, but a lot of times, the old ways are the best ways," offered Monk.

Bruno slid a fresh tape into his camera.

"You think one of those things is really going to fall for that . . ." Charles's voice trailed off, and he tossed his head in the direction of the hole.

"Absolutely. The lycanthropes, or those *things*, as you call them, are also human, which means they have human intelligence. For that reason, I don't presume they would crawl inside a regular trap just for a piece of meat on a string."

Charles pressed his lips together and shrugged, as if to say, "Whatever."

"Are you ready?" Monk asked.

Bruno lifted the camera onto his shoulder, pressed his right eye against the eyepiece, and said, "Speed."

Charles gave the doctor the thumbs up.

Monk remained motionless for a count of three and then began placing cedar branches across the top of the hole.

"As a scientist, it is my goal to capture one of these amazing creatures alive so that I might be able to study it in a controlled scientific environment and hopefully unlock the secrets of its unique shape shifting abilities."

Bruno kept the camera focused on Monk but pulled his eye away from the eyepiece to look at Charles.

"For it's only through scientific research and investigation that the sheer magnitude of my discovery can be fully realized – and the benefits can be shared with all of humankind."

When Charles looked over Bruno rolled his eyes.

·•·

The air was sweet with the smell of pine needles and humus. It had rained overnight and the entire forest seemed fresh and alive. It was the perfect place for the pack to be after a hard day among humans.

The four wolves ran, bounding between the trees with reckless abandon, feeling nature's energy flowing through them and rejuvenating them with a strength few others would ever know. Noble led the way, guiding them along the path they all knew well. It would take them to the town of Redstone and back again, a round-trip of over three miles, which they could all easily run in less than twenty minutes.

Noble was fastest, his wolfen form possessing just the right size and proportions for speed. Argus was strongest, but most of his energy went to moving his massive body, and he was slower because of it. Harlan and Tora often ran neck-and-neck. Tora was slightly bigger than Harlan so she had a longer stride, but being a female, she also had less muscle mass than her little brother. And because of his smaller size, Harlan could sometimes dart ahead of the rest with a sudden burst of speed, or find ways through the forest the others couldn't manage – like now.

Harlan had run ahead of the rest, bounding through a stand of young spruce and cedar trees off to the side of the path that would have stopped the others dead in their tracks. He gave a little howl to taunt the others and to make sure they knew he was out front and in the lead.

Noble stepped up his pace and began to close the gap.

Argus did his best to keep up, panting noticeably with his tongue lolling limply at the side of his maw.

Tora was falling behind. She didn't like being last, especially when Harlan was the one leading the way. If he was first to arrive at the end of the trail and she was last, she'd never hear the end of it. She couldn't let that happen.

Tora dashed to the left, leaping off the trail and into a small clearing. She knew a shortcut and if she timed it right, she'd arrive at the end of the trail ahead of the others with enough time to change form and get comfortable enough to ask them all, "What took you so long?" without too much panting.

She could see the others bounding off to her right for several moments before they became obscured by the trees. Then she listened to them fading into the forest, snapping twigs and brushing past branches as they still raced against each other to see who would finish first.

Won't they be surprised to see me waiting, she thought. *All dressed and hardly breaking a sweat.* The thought drove her harder and faster through the clearing. She was almost at the edge of it. Beyond the open stretch of land lay another stand of trees with a path all its own. She'd be through it in minutes and then . . .

And then the ground fell away beneath her.

It was a strange sort of feeling, one she'd never experienced before. One moment she was running through the forest with hard-packed ground beneath her paws, the next the ground was gone and she was falling.

Her left shoulder hit first. Then her head snapped left, striking something solid. The rest of her body followed in an instant, her middle and haunches slamming into a wall of unforgiving earth, bending and crumpling for what seemed like an eternity, but was really no longer than a fraction of a second.

Suddenly silence – except for a strange ringing in her ears. Tora slowly opened her eyes. She was on her side. Her shoulders ached, her limbs too, but there were no sharp pains to suggest she'd broken anything. Just count-less dull throbs and a fog inside her head that made it seem as if a veil had been pulled over her eyes.

She was lying in a pit, a hole in the blackness above her revealing that the blue afternoon sky had clouded over slightly. The walls of the hole were high, too high to allow her to crawl out, even if she felt up to the task. She closed her eyes and rested. Maybe in a few minutes she could try to leap. Yes, after a few minutes of rest she'd be stronger.

Just then, voices.

Tora's first thought was that they belonged to Noble, Argus and Harlan, and she was about to call out to them when she caught an unfamiliar scent.

Men.

The voices came closer.

"You got it on tape, right?" said the first voice.

"Yes." That one sounded annoyed.

"And the snap and crackle of the branches." The first voice again.

"Of course." A different voice this time. A third man.

"Get a shot inside the trap."

No more words, just the sound of someone approach-ing and the faint hum of something with an electric motor.

The hole was suddenly bathed in light. She looked up into the bright white circle and was momentarily blinded. Then the light shifted, and she could make out the sil-houette of a man standing over her with a camera on his shoulder. He was there filming her for several seconds before moving aside and returning her to darkness.

"Now what?" the second voice, the man with the camera, said.

"What do you think? We get it out of there."

Two men peered over the edge of the hole. She could see them a bit more clearly now that the bright light was gone, but with the brighter sky behind them, their heads were still little more than silhouettes.

She snarled at them, baring her teeth.

"Why don't you show us how it's done?" said the third voice.

Silence for a while.

Then another man was leaning over the edge of the hole. The man who belonged to the first voice.

She growled long and low.

He laughed in response, then disappeared from the edge of the hole, reappearing a moment later with a long hollow tube in his hands. He raised the tube to his lips.

"Hey, come on," said the second voice.

"I won't hurt it," said the first.

Tora heard a *whoosh* of air, like a pressure valve letting go. And there was suddenly a sharp pain in her right haunch. She glanced over and saw the feathered end of a dart nestled in the midst of her thick gray fur.

She curled around and gnawed at the dart for a moment, trying to pull it out with her teeth. But as the seconds passed, removing the dart seemed less and less important to her. After a while, she didn't care anymore. The world was getting darker. And all she wanted to do was sleep.

Chapter 4

Harlan couldn't believe it. The end of the path was in sight and he was still out front and in the lead. A quick look behind him confirmed it. Noble and Argus were several strides back, keeping pace, but not gaining on him. And Tora, well she must have been even farther behind.

Finally, thought Harlan. *I don't have to be last, or the smallest, or the weakest anymore.*

He stopped at the base of the large cedar, near where the forest ended, and let out a yelping howl of joy. Soon the others finished their run as well, congratulating Harlan by rising up on their hind legs and giving him a yelp.

Harlan was the first to change his shape into human form. "I won, I won," he said. "I was here first!"

Noble completed his change. "Congratulations, Harlan."

Followed by Argus. "Yeah, way to go."

Harlan looked at his brother closely a moment, then said, "You guys didn't let me win, did you?"

Both shook there heads.

Harlan pumped his fist into the air. "All right!"

As they began getting dressed, Noble took a moment to look around. "What about Tora?"

"No way she was here before me," Harlan said, eager not to have his victory tainted in any way.

"Then where is she?"

Argus turned around and began walking back along the path in the direction they'd come. "She couldn't be that far behind."

"Maybe she got lost," suggested Harlan.

Noble shook his head. "Not likely. She knows the forest as well, maybe even better, than we do."

"We have to look for her," stated Argus.

Noble turned to face Harlan. "See if you can catch –" he began to say, but stopped in midsentence when he saw that Harlan had already changed back into wolf form and was sniffing along the path trying to pick up Tora's scent.

"Was she by this way?" Argus asked.

Harlan shook his head.

"Right," said Noble. "Then we'll just have to retrace our steps until we figure out where she went."

Moments later, the three brother wolves were headed back into the forest to find their sister.

•◆•

"Not so tough with a mix of xylazine and ketamine inside you, eh?" mumbled Doctor Monk.

He was down in the hole Bruno had dug, trying to roll the body of the wolf onto a sling he'd made from a bedsheet borrowed from their motel room. Although the wolf had been drugged, moving it into position wasn't all that easy. The wolf had to weigh somewhere between a hundred and a hundred and twenty pounds. That wasn't all that heavy, but it wasn't like the wolf had come with a set of handles.

"Could one of you two get down here and help me," the doctor said.

Neither of the men moved.

"If I come down there to help you," said Bruno, "Who's going to operate the camera?"

Charles nodded in agreement. "And if I come down, who will record your words for posterity?"

Monk seemed to considered their arguments, then nodded. "Right."

Above him, it sounded as if one or both of the men had laughed under their breath. Monk ignored them and redoubled his efforts, grabbing the wolf by the scruff of the neck with one hand and by the tail with the other, and heaved the prone animal into place on the sling with a single awkward movement.

The wolf landed hard on its side, causing the air to whoosh from its lungs in something that sounded like a growl.

Monk instinctively jumped back, slamming his head against the earthen wall behind him.

Bruno and Charles both laughed out loud.

Monk looked up slowly, eyes narrowed and teeth clenched. "Laugh all you want now," he said. "But I'll be the one laughing last – all the way to the bank."

The two men fell silent.

Monk raised the corners of the sling and tied them off with a rope. Then he extended his right hand. "Get me out of here."

Charles reached down and pulled the doctor out of the hole.

Moments later, Monk was straddling the hole and lifting the still unconscious wolf up out of the ground.

"Go get the truck," he said.

•◆•

Harlan stopped in midstep. After retracing their route back through the forest for nearly twenty minutes, he'd finally found Tora's scent.

Behind him, Noble and Argus also froze.

Harlan sniffed the path more carefully, imprinting Tora's scent on his mind, then slowly turned to the right, following the scent as it trailed off the path. Obviously this was where she'd left the path, to take a shortcut perhaps, or maybe to investigate something in the woods.

Noble and Argus sniffed along the path, no doubt recognizing Tora's scent for themselves.

Harlan turned in the direction Tora had gone, then followed the scent as it lead away from the path and into the clearing.

His brothers fell in behind him.

Not more than twenty paces into the clearing, Harlan felt the hair along his back stand up on end. There were other scents here that didn't belong. Plastic, motor oil, and coffee . . . and men. Two, maybe three of them, walking all around this area . . . back and forth and in circles.

Harlan slowly moved toward the center of the clearing and the hair all over his body bristled as Tora's scent suddenly became tinged with the unmistakable smell of fear. Then without warning, Harlan's front right paw lost its footing and he had to scramble back to keep himself from falling forward.

The three wolves stood still, looking at the ground.

In his rush to get back, Harlan had pushed aside a cedar bough, revealing a large black hole beneath it.

They moved in for a closer inspection.

"It's a trap," Noble said after changing into human form and pulling several boughs away from the hole with his hand.

Argus bared his teeth and growled angrily under his breath.

"Tora fell in there," Harlan said, moving branches away and dropping down into the hole.

"Was she hurt?" Noble asked.

Harlan shook his head as he examined the earthen walls and floor. "There's no blood. I didn't smell any either."

"Well, that's something, at least."

"She was scared, that's for sure," Harlan explained. "But I don't think they hurt her. I sensed a chemical smell before. They probably drugged her and pulled her out.

Then they loaded her into a van or truck that was parked nearby."

"So she's gone?"

Harlan said nothing for a few moments, thinking things through. He had the most technical mind of the three of them, and loved being challenged by puzzles and other problems of logic – like this one.

"She's not gone," he said. "Not gone far, anyway."

"How do you know?" Noble asked, not doubting his brother, but curious about his path of reasoning.

"They covered up the trap before they left. That means they either don't want anyone to know they were here, or they're hoping to capture another one of us."

Argus growled again, louder this time.

"So they'll be coming back."

Harlan nodded, reaching up so Noble could help lift him out of the hole. "Eventually, sure. But who knows what they might do to Tora in the meantime."

"Do you think you can find her?" Noble asked.

Harlan didn't answer. He had already changed back into his wolf form and was busy sniffing the perimeter of the clearing trying to pick up the scent of the men who had captured his sister. It didn't take long for him to find it. He yelped once to get his brothers' attention, and then he was gone, bounding through the forest.

Headed toward Redstone.

Chapter 5

It wasn't all that difficult to follow the men who had taken Tora from the forest. The truck they'd driven was old and burned a lot of oil, leaving a trail for Harlan that was so distinct, it was as if someone had painted a line on the roadway for him to follow.

The line led them to the Redstone Inn, where they found a ten-year-old cube van parked around the back with the words MONK COMMUNICATIONS written on the side in big black letters. Obviously, Tora had been captured by the geneticist Ranger Brock had told them about and was being held inside the man's company van. The van was backed up to the door of a room on the ground floor and there were several men moving back and forth between the motel room and the van.

As the three wolves sat watching from the woods behind the inn, all three pairs of ears pricked up at the sound of another wolf's call of distress. It was a long tapered moan coming from the inside of the van, and hearing it gave Noble mixed emotions. On the one hand it pained him to know Tora was being held captive, perhaps even suffering somehow. On the other hand, at least it was proof she was alive.

He turned to the other two wolves and signaled for them to follow him. There was about fifty yards of clearing between the woods and the van. Off to one side of the van was an SUV, while farther away on the other side was a minivan. If they could use the SUV as a form of cover, it might be possible to get Tora out without being seen.

Noble led the wolves around the edge of the woods to the point closest to the SUV. After watching the men for several minutes, it was clear that there were only three of them. The older one was obviously Doctor Monk, and of the other two, only one was much of a physical threat to them, providing the men didn't have any weapons.

Noble changed his form so he could speak to the others and make it clear to them what he wanted to do.

"We'll wait until all three of them are in the motel room," he said in a whisper, "then we'll rush the van. Argus, you take the room door and make sure no one comes out."

Argus raised his head and gave a silent yelp.

"Harlan, you stand watch. If you see anyone approaching, or any other kind of danger, sound the alarm."

Harlan nodded his wolfen head.

"I'll check out the van. If Tora's in there, I'll try to get her out."

Argus and Harlan's eyes were fixed on the van.

Noble changed back into wolfen form and joined watch.

The sun was starting to set behind the Nechako Mountains, and the sky was a mix of deep red and purple hues. The parking lot outside the inn was getting dark, and the lights spotting the lot would be coming on in minutes. If they didn't move soon, the lot would be bathed in light, making it that much harder for them to get to Tora without being seen.

Noble counted two men in the room, the other in the van. If the one in the van didn't move in the next few minutes, they'd have no other choice but to chase him away to get to Tora. Noble didn't want to hurt anybody, but if it was a choice between his sister and one of the men who was holding her captive, there was really no choice to be made – the human would have to go.

He was preparing to move in closer when he heard the sound of a vehicle approaching. Noble and the others sat back on their haunches and waited.

The car had a lighted sign on its roof. The men had ordered a pizza.

Patiently, the wolves watched as the delivery man got out of the car and approached the motel room. He knocked on the door, waited, then exchanged the pizza box and bag in his hand for some money. Moments later the delivery man was back in his car and driving off the lot.

One of the men came out of the motel room, knocked on the back of the van, and went back inside. Before the motel room door even closed, the third man was scampering out of the van into the room.

This was it. Without a moment's hesitation, Noble darted from the woods toward the SUV. He stopped there a moment, waiting for the others to catch up. The moment they were all together, Noble bolted for the van, with the sound of his brothers' paws clicking against the pavement following close behind him.

The back of the van was closed, but not locked. Still, the door was inaccessible to a wolf, and Noble had to change form in order to turn the latch and swing open the heavy barn-style door.

As he worked on the door, Noble glanced over at Argus, who had his body placed in front of the door to the motel room, leaning heavily against it to make sure no one would get out. Harlan was out of sight, probably positioned in front of the van with a good view of the motel and the surrounding parking lot.

In seconds, the door of the van was swinging open. Tora was in the van but trapped inside a cage made of heavy gauge steel with an equally impressive steel lock on its door.

Noble stepped inside the van, partially closing the door behind him. "Tora," he said, putting his hand up against the cage, "Are you all right? Have they hurt you?"

Tora shook her head from side to side, then rubbed her muzzle against his hand. It was obvious she was weak, despite her assertion that she was fine. There were several electrodes attached to her body that led into what seemed like some sort of diagnostic machine. But the longer Noble remained in the van, the more he was aware of the smell of ozone in the air . . . and burnt fur. He looked more closely at the electrodes attached to Tora's body and saw that the fur around each one had turned black.

The realization hit Noble like a punch to the gut. They weren't monitoring Tora, they were giving her electrical shocks to see if they could make her change her form. Tora looked haggard, but she was still a wolf. If the electro-shocks had done anything to her, they had brightened the streak down her back.

Noble made a futile attempt to unlock the door, but it was secure. Given time and space, someone like Argus might be able to spread the bars and free Tora. But Noble wasn't nearly as strong as his bigger brother, and the cage was wedged into the van pretty tightly. He glanced around for a key, or maybe a tool to cut the lock or bend the bars of the cage, but there was nothing in the van but books, computers, microscopes, and video tapes.

They couldn't rescue Tora now, but they could come back better prepared and try again.

Just then Harlan began yelping out in the parking lot.

Through the crack in the open van door, Noble noticed that the lights had come on in one of the motel rooms.

He turned to Tora. "Stay strong," he said. "We'll be back." She licked his hand, then lay down inside the cage.

Noble was out of the van a moment later.

Argus was still pressed up against the door to the motel room, but the moment he saw Noble, he straightened up and began to run.

Harlan joined up with them at the edge of the woods, and together the three wolves leaped into the forest.

Behind them, people were converging in the motel parking lot wondering what all the commotion was about.

•◆•

"I say we go back there," Argus said through partially clenched teeth. "And take her!" He was in werewolf form, halfway between wolf and human. His face was long and narrow, and tufts of thick fur surrounded his eyes and the sides of his face. The rest of his face and all of his body – a mass of rippling, bulging muscles – was covered by a coat of gray fur that seemed to bristle with anger at the thought of Tora's predicament.

Noble put a hand up to calm his brother.

Argus was having none of it.

"I didn't want to run," he said, the tips of his fangs wet and glistening beneath the dim light of the moon. "I was ready to fight . . . all of them."

"As what? A werewolf?" Noble's voice was calm and even. Argus had been snarling for several minutes, but Noble hadn't let it affect him. This was Argus's way of dealing with his anger and frustration, and if it took him all night to calm down, then that's how long they would wait.

"Of course," Argus spat. "I could take down four men by myself. You and Harlan could handle the others, and then we could get Tora out of that . . . that . . . cage!"

The flesh on his arm seemed to roil beneath his fur at the very thought of one of his kind being locked up, and by humans no less.

Noble was silent for almost half a minute before he said, "And then what? We just go on living as we have been, as if nothing happened?"

"Yes."

Noble looked over at Harlan to see if he was in agreement with Argus. Harlan shook his head slightly.

Noble turned to face Argus. "You know that could never happen."

Argus suddenly seemed smaller, his anger lessened.

"If we killed any of those men, they'd come after us and hunt us down . . . with guns and cameras." A pause. "We'd have to remain human for the rest of our lives."

Harlan groaned at the thought.

Argus, now close to human form, hung his head low and turned it slightly away from Noble, as if he knew his brother was right, but wasn't about to admit it in so many words.

"Right now, all that has happened is that this Doctor Monk has caught himself a wolf and the other members of this wolf's pack came nosing around looking for it. That's all."

Argus raised his head. "So what do we do, then? Nothing?"

"No, not nothing," Noble said, turning to face the direction they'd come. "What the doctor has done is not only unjust, I believe it's also illegal."

"He doesn't strike me as the type to worry about stuff like that," offered Harlan.

"Obviously not," said Noble. "But there are plenty of humans who do worry about such things. In fact it's their job to make sure that such things don't happen."

"Like Ranger Brock," said Harlan.

Argus's face brightened.

"Exactly. This is a human problem. We have to give the humans the chance to make things right."

"And then?" Argus wanted to know.

"And then, we'll see."

Chapter 6

They were huddled around the living room in Ranger Brock's home. He was seated in his usual chair by the fireplace dressed in his bathrobe. Phyllis was in the kitchen brewing a fresh pot of coffee for her husband and making hot chocolate for the three boys.

"And he's at the Redstone Inn?" asked the ranger.

"The van says MONK COMMUNICATIONS right on the side in big letters," said Noble.

"You can't miss it," Harlan added.

"She's all right, though?" The ranger's face was a mask of concern.

Noble nodded. "For now, yes. But who knows how long he'll be hanging around."

Argus stepped forward. "You have to do something. Fast!"

Ranger Brock nodded slightly, then turned and picked up the telephone on the table next to him. He dialed a number he knew by heart.

Phyllis entered the room, carrying a tray with five mugs and a plate of homemade cookies on it. "They didn't mistreat her, did they?" she asked.

Noble didn't answer right away, wondering if he should tell her about the electrodes he saw attached to Tora's body and Monk's attempts to force her to change her shape. After all, the ranger and his wife were in an odd situation here. Ranger Brock had a duty to prevent wild animals from being taken from the forest. While that was significant enough, the wolf in question was also his adopted daughter, only he could never admit to such a thing. Ever.

"No," Noble said at last. "She's in good shape."

"Oh, that's a relief," Phyllis said, placing an open hand over her heart, as if to help calm its beating.

Ranger Brock sat up straight in his chair. "Hello, constable," he said. "This is Ranger Garrett Brock . . . that's right, I'm responsible for the area around Redstone. I'd like to speak to the sergeant on duty, if I could."

Another pause.

Noble took a sip of his hot chocolate and a bite of one of Phyllis's cookies. It was chocolate chip, made from a batter she'd bought during a fundraising campaign at the school. As he chewed on it, he looked around the room.

Argus had several cookies in his hand and was reaching for yet another one. Harlan held his mug close to his body with both hands, as if the hot chocolate might warm his body without him even drinking it.

Phyllis just stared at her husband.

"Evening Sergeant Martin. . . . Good, how are you?" Another pause. "I've been made aware of a problem that I think I might need your assistance with."

Ranger Brock leaned right, moving a little closer to the phone, and began explaining what had happened to Tora. He relayed the story exactly the way it had been told to him, although he said he'd been tipped off by an anonymous caller, and he constantly referred to Tora as simply a wolf.

"Okay, good, thank you," he said in quick succession, signaling the end of the conversation. "I'll meet you there." He hung up the phone and glanced around the room. Four wide-eyed faces waited eagerly to hear some news. "The police are on their way to the Redstone Inn as we speak."

Noble let out a sigh of relief. Everyone did.

"I have to meet them there," the ranger said, getting up from his chair. "They'll be turning the wolf . . . I mean Tora, over to me when they're done with Doctor Monk."

"We'll come with you," said Argus.

The ranger's face suddenly looked pained. "People might wonder why I brought my family out at night just to pick up a wolf."

Harlan's shoulders sagged visibly.

"I'll drive them," Phyllis offered. "You can't blame a ranger's wife for stopping to check on her husband on her way home from the grocery store, now can you?"

Ranger Brock let out a laugh under his breath.

"All right," said Harlan.

Noble turned for the door. "Let's go."

•◆•

The RCMP waited for Ranger Brock to arrive before they knocked on the door of Doctor Monk's room. Sergeant Martin, with two constables behind him, hammered on the door with a closed fist. He waited a few moments, then tried it again, harder this time.

"Who the hell is banging on my door?"

The man in the room sounded annoyed.

"Police!" said the sergeant. "Open up!"

There was movement on the other side of the door, like a chain sliding open and the lock being undone.

The sergeant was about to pound on the door again, but it suddenly opened a crack, just wide enough for an old man to peer out of the room at the assembled police.

"Is there a problem, officer?" he asked.

Ranger Brock recognized the old man as Doctor Monk. His hair was a bit disheveled and his face was lined with wrinkles that makeup obviously did wonders to hide when he appeared on camera, but it was definitely him.

"Are you Doctor Edward Monk?"

The door opened a bit wider. The man nodded.

"We've received a report . . ." At this point Sergeant

Martin turned and nodded in Ranger Brock's direction. "that you've captured a wolf and are holding it captive inside a truck."

Monk looked shocked, as if he were surprised and offended by what the sergeant had just told him.

Ranger Brock's heart sank. Since the cube van the boys had said was parked in the lot wasn't there at the moment, chances were good that Monk had already transported Tora out of the area and would simply deny knowing anything about any wolf.

But to the ranger's surprised he said, "Yes, that's right."

Even Sergeant Martin looked surprised by the admission. "It's a wild animal, sir," he said. "I'm going to have to ask you to hand it over to the ranger so he can return it to the wild." After a pause, he added, "Where it belongs."

Monk smiled at that, saying nothing for the longest time.

For some reason, Monk's response made Ranger Brock uncomfortable. It was an odd sort of smile, phony and smug and maybe just a little bit evil, as if Monk knew something no one else did.

"I can't do that," Monk said at last.

"Why's that?"

"It's no ordinary wolf."

The sergeant sighed, obviously losing patience with the old man. He glanced over at Ranger Brock and then turned his head to face the doctor. "Yeah, what's so special about it?"

"It can change its shape from wolf to human form, and back again –"

The sergeant had obviously heard enough. "Look," he said, cutting Monk off in midsentence. "What you've done is against the law. Period. I'm going to give you a chance to make things right. You turn the animal over to the ranger here, and if it hasn't been harmed, then I won't arrest you or take you to jail."

Monk smiled and nodded, but it was obvious that he and the sergeant were not on the same wavelength. Even looking like a mess and dressed in a ratty bathrobe, Doctor Monk was still able to exude an air of superiority that was at the same time intimidating and annoying.

"I understand your position, officer," Monk said with a respectful tone that was still very much condescending. "But you really don't understand. This is a once in a life-time find. This wolf could unlock secrets that might save millions from illness and disease –"

The sergeant cut him off again. "You either turn over the animal now, or go to jail."

Monk was silent for several moments, considering his options. "Since I won't be turning the wolf over to you, and you seem intent on arresting me, might I be so bold as to ask that I make my phone call now. I assure you I won't be calling my lawyer, and when I'm done, this matter will likely be resolved without you having to arrest me."

The sergeant thought it over as if the thought of resolving this matter tonight was a tempting offer.

"One call!" he said.

Monk pulled a cell phone from the pocket of his bathrobe and dialed a number.

Long distance.

•—•—•

By the time Phyllis and the boys had arrived at the Redstone Inn, Ranger Brock's 4 x 4 was parked in the lot along with three RCMP police cruisers. Two of the cruisers had their lights flashing, and a crowd of people had gathered around the edges of the lot to see what was going on. Not much of anything at the moment. Or so it seemed.

"The van's not here," Noble noted after they'd come to a stop and Phyllis had turned off the engine of the family's Jeep Cherokee.

"Tora was in it?" Phyllis asked.

"Yes."

"Oh no."

Harlan was looking out the back of the car at the highway. "What do you think happened to it?"

"I have a feeling we're about to find out," said Argus, pointing at Ranger Brock who was on his way over to the car.

When he could see the features of the ranger's face, Noble instinctively knew the news wasn't going to be good.

Noble rolled down the passenger-side window.

"Where's Tora?" Phyllis said.

Ranger Brock leaned in closer to the window. "She's in Monk's van . . . Safe." He added the last word as if he'd suddenly remembered who he was talking to.

"She's not here?"

The ranger shook his head.

"What's happened?" Noble said, making sure he kept his voice even and strong.

"It seems Doctor Monk knows people in high places."

Noble didn't understand. "What's that supposed to mean?"

"He made a few phone calls to people who have a lot of power."

"Like who?" Argus wanted to know.

"Like the Premier of British Columbia for starters. Then the provincial Forests Minister called him back, and the federal Minister of the Environment. He even got a call from one of the top brass at the RCMP."

"In Vancouver?"

"No," Ranger Brock shook his head. "In Ottawa."

None of this sounded very good for Tora's release. Noble felt as if all of the strength had suddenly been sucked from his body. He felt weak and helpless, and judging by the way he was leaning up against the car – as if it were helping to keep him upright and on his feet – Ranger Brock was feeling the very same way.

"So, they're just letting him take her?"

Ranger Brock quickly shook his head. "No, that's not happening yet."

Yet. The word seemed to echo in Noble's mind.

"Then what *is* happening?" Phyllis asked, a tinge of fear edging her voice.

"Monk says the wolf is a special case and he's working on getting permission to take her out of the wild so he can . . ." The ranger slowed here, obviously having trouble getting the words out. "So he can . . . conduct some experiments –"

"Aw c'mon." Argus said.

"No way!" Harlan exclaimed.

Ranger Brock put up his hands as if in surrender. "But none of that has happened yet. He's not going anywhere for the moment."

"What about Tora?" Phyllis's voice cracked with worry.

"Monk is bringing her back here so she can be kept under guard."

"But –"

The ranger raised just his right hand this time. "I've already suggested that I hold her until a decision is made, but Monk refused. He claims I'll let the animal escape."

Noble sighed. That's exactly what Ranger Brock would have done. Obviously, Doctor Monk was very smart and cunning . . . for a human. But he wasn't as cunning as a wolf, let alone three of them.

Just then, a pair of headlights swept across the parking lot. Ranger Brock turned to face the light and an expression of recognition appeared on his face.

Noble turned and saw two men in the Monk Communications van pull into the lot. He wanted to jump out of the Jeep and rush to Tora's side, but this wasn't the time or place for such action. No doubt Argus had a similar idea in mind, only his thoughts were probably more along the lines of tearing apart any human who stood between him and his sister's freedom.

"You better go home now," said Ranger Brock. "I'll stay with Tora through the night to make sure she's all right." He forced himself to smile. "It's the least they allowed me."

Noble wanted to stay but knew there was no point to it. Tora would be safe in Ranger Brock's hands. But he wasn't about to leave without saying something. "Don't let anything happen to her."

"Not a chance. Besides, the Forests Minister won't be here until late tomorrow afternoon, so there won't be a decision one way or another until tomorrow night at the earliest."

The ranger's words churned Noble's stomach. From what he'd said, there was a real chance that the humans might allow Tora to be taken from them. Noble couldn't let that happen. He had to come up with a plan. Just in case the human world failed them.

Chapter 7

Noble, Argus, and Harlan all went to school the next morning, but the last thing on any of their minds was schoolwork. Harlan breezed through science class without saying a word. Argus completely ignored it when Brent Romanuk called him "Freaky-Eye Beastie Boy." And Noble told Julie Resnick he was busy Friday night, even when she hinted that her parents would be away til early Saturday morning.

All they could think about was Tora. Was she all right? Would they eventually let her go? What would they do if Ranger Brock couldn't bring her home?

Noble wanted to work on the problem. Unfortunately he had to get through a day of school before he could spend any time on a plan. As a result, school had never been so long and tedious. Noble thought the day might never come to an end. And it was only lunch period.

The three brothers gathered in the cafeteria, eating their lunches in silence while the rest of the student body roared with chatter around them.

Finally, after he'd finished his two sandwiches, Noble said, "I called Phyllis this morning."

Argus and Harlan leaned in closer, eager for news.

"No change."

They rolled back in disappointment.

"Hi guys," said a voice.

Noble turned to see Michael Martin standing at the end of their table.

"Mind if I sit down?"

Noble shrugged. He liked Michael, and so did his brothers, but they were always wary of allowing humans into their inner circle. Michael Martin seemed like the kind of person who could understand and accept what they were, but they could never be sure about something like that. Things like friendship, opinion, and loyalty were qualities that could change in humans as often as the direction of the wind changed in the forest. They all wanted Michael Martin to be their friend, and they *needed* a human they could trust and confide in, but Michael would have to prove himself before they accepted him as a member of the pack.

Argus pulled his books to the center of the table to make room for their friend.

Michael pulled out his lunch and began eating a sandwich, slowly realizing that the others weren't speaking. "Cats got your tongues?" he said.

The three brothers said nothing.

"Okay . . ." He took another bite of his sandwich.

After a few minutes of silence Michael said, "By the way, where's Tora? She usually eats with you guys, doesn't she?"

Noble quickly looked over at Michael at the mention of his sister, thinking Michael might know something. Michael, after all, was the son of Sergeant Martin, and his father had been the police officer who confronted Doctor Monk the night before. But even if his father had told Michael what had happened, there was no way he would make the connection between the wolf in Doctor Monk's possession and Tora being missing.

"She's not here!" said Argus, forcefully.

"Hey, I'm just asking."

Noble looked at Argus, gesturing to him that maybe he should tone it down a little. Then he turned to Michael and smiled. "She wasn't feeling well this morning," he said. "She decided to stay home and rest. She'll be back by the end of the week."

"Good as new," interjected Harlan.

"Yes," Noble agreed. "Good as new."

"Maybe I should give her a call," said Michael. "Or better still, I could drop by the house."

Noble shook his head. He hated to lie to Michael about anything because, of all the students at the school, Michael

Martin was the most accepting of the pack, even when their behavior could be characterized as *odd*. Like now.

And Noble couldn't be sure, but there were times when he thought Michael suspected that the four of them were lycanthropes. At other times, however, he acted as if he didn't have a clue about their secret . . . or even life in general. But probably the most endearing feature about Michael Martin was that he had taken a liking to Tora, and she was rather fond of him as well. Michael probably would have asked her out on a date by now if he wasn't a little wary of her three brothers who – truth be told – could become quite intimidating under the right circumstances.

"That's not a good idea," Noble said in response to Michael's suggested visit.

"Why not?" asked Michael.

"She's . . . resting!" Noble said, trying to keep the emotion from his voice but failing miserably. He took a deep breath and continued. "She's not feeling up to seeing or talking to anyone right now."

"Okay, okay, I just thought she might like to hear from a friend."

Noble was going to say something, but Argus spoke before he had the chance to.

"Believe me," Argus said, putting one of his large hands over Michael Martin's decidedly smaller one. It was an odd gesture for two teenage boys, but it spoke volumes about friendship and trust. "I don't think there are many things Tora would want more right now than to hear a kind word from you and to talk about the weather . . . but she can't. Not for a little while anyway."

Argus pulled his hand away from Michael's. No one said anything for several long moments.

Finally Michael's eyes narrowed slightly and he said, "There's something big going on right now, isn't there?"

What to say? Noble wondered. Do you say "No" and lie to a close friend, or do you say "Yes" and trust that your friend is smart enough to figure it out on his own, and then be able to keep what he knows to himself.

Noble looked around the table at his brothers, then turned to Michael and said, "Yes, there is."

Chapter 8

After school, Noble, Argus, and Harlan decided to go straight to the Redstone Inn to check on Tora. The motel looked quiet with only a few cars in the parking lot belonging to guests and the police, as well as Ranger Brock's 4 x 4.

The cube van was still there too, parked in the same spot as the night before. Ranger Brock was standing behind the van sipping coffee out of a paper cup. When he saw the boys standing at the edge of the lot, he acknowledged them with a wave, then walked toward them. As he neared, the look on his face told the story. The situation had gotten worse.

"Hey boys, how was your day?"

"Okay, how's Tora?" Argus said, asking the question so fast he almost ignored the ranger's greeting.

"She's fine."

Noble didn't like the way the ranger had answered the question. *Fine* was a word people used when they didn't want to rock the boat. "Is she still in the van?"

The ranger nodded. "Yes."

"Why?"

Ranger Brock frowned and let out a sigh. Noble knew right away that he wasn't going to like the ranger's answer.

"Monk got permission to take her."

"Permission?" said Argus. From his tone it was obvious that Argus found the very idea insulting. "From who?"

"The federal Ministry of the Environment."

"To take her where?" asked Harlan.

"He's got access to a research facility at the zoo in Vancouver."

"The zoo!" The veins in Argus's neck were standing out in high relief against the flesh of his neck. "When is this supposed to happen?"

"The ministry has sent a man up from Victoria today with all the paperwork. He should be here by this evening. After that, Monk will be free to go. He'll probably be gone by morning."

Noble shook his head in disbelief. "You can't let that happen."

The ranger closed his eyes a moment, then opened them to look at Noble. "I already got a call from the head of the Forest Service and was told to assist Doctor Monk . . . with anything he needs."

Argus shook his head in disbelief. "You can't be serious."

"No, it's true," the ranger said, crushing his coffee cup in his hand. "I'm afraid the system's failed our Tora."

"But there has to be *something* you can do?"

The ranger was silent for several moments, then said, "Legally, my hands are tied. I can't do anything without jeopardizing my job and your lives in the forest. And, practically speaking, there are just too many people watching this place for me to do anything illegal."

"So you're just going to let them take Tora . . . to the *zoo*?"

The ranger shook his head, then looked at the three boys as if he knew he was about to touch on a delicate subject. "I was thinking if Tora changed form . . . became human, Monk would have no choice but to let her go."

"Then he'd know our secret," said Harlan. "He'd have irrefutable proof of it . . . Tora's life would be hell."

"All our lives would be hell," echoed Argus.

"But we'd have her back," said Ranger Brock. "And you'd all be together again."

"No!" said Noble.

Everyone looked at Noble, waiting for him to elaborate.

"What your proposing suggests that it's all right to take a wolf from its family for research purposes, but not a human . . ."

"Hey, that's right," Harlan interjected.

"I can't agree with that," Noble continued.

Ranger Brock said nothing, but there was no mistaking the look of shame on his face. "You have another idea?"

Noble nodded. "Yes."

"Want to tell me about it?"

He thought about it a moment, then said, "No. Maybe it's better if I didn't."

•-•-

"So what *do* you have in mind?" Argus said as they walked along the road that led home.

Harlan took a few quick steps to catch up to the other two. "We could put the word out in town. I'm sure if people knew what was going on, there'd be plenty of tree-huggers out to protest."

Argus gave his little brother a playful slap on the back. "None of those people live in Redstone," he said. "They have to bring them in from out of town, like from Victoria and Vancouver . . . sometimes even Toronto."

"It's a good idea," Noble said. "But Argus is right. Protesters need time to organize. By the time they get here, Tora will be gone."

"What about the press, then?" Harlan continued, still wanting to make a contribution, maybe even come up with *the* plan to free Tora.

Noble nodded. "That might slow Monk down, but it wouldn't stop him. And it would bring a lot of unwanted attention onto Tora. If she ever changed form in the spotlight, it would be over for her. Over for all of us."

"The zoo!" Argus spat.

"Then what do *you* think we should do?" Harlan asked.

Noble remained silent, deep in thought.

"We can't count on help from any humans, that's for sure." Argus's voice was taut with coiled anger.

"They're not all bad," Harlan interjected.

Almost immediately Argus's expression softened. They all owed their lives to Ranger Brock and his wife. As much as the ranger wanted to, he was unable to do anything in this situation because of a complex net of rules, regulations, and people with power. If anything, the members of the pack understood hierarchy. Ranger Brock had some power in the forest, but there were many others higher up on the ladder who had more power than he did. Much more.

Still, that didn't mean *all* humans were bad, that all humans couldn't be trusted.

Noble broke into a run.

"Where you goin'?" asked Harlan, hurrying to keep pace.

"I need to call Michael Martin."

"How come?"

"I think he can help us."

Chapter 9

Bruno was at work inside the van, replacing the tape that had just been in the camera with the last blank tape he had. He'd gone through six of them in the last day, each one filled with footage of the wolf sitting up, the wolf lying down, or the wolf fast asleep. Some of the footage could be used for the show they were putting together – mostly of the wolf moving around, changing position, that sort of thing – but the hours and hours of the wolf sleeping were a waste of tape.

He decided to check the tape that had just finished to see if there was anything useful on it. If there was anything good, he'd hang onto it, but if it was just more of the same, he could put it back into the camera and record over it if he needed to.

He slid the tape into one of the larger decks in the back of the van and hit the *rewind* button. The deck made a few clicking sounds, then began to slowly rewind the tape. After a few minutes, the hum of the machine quickened pace as it raced to get back to the beginning. Then all of a sudden the machine came to a halt.

The sound of the stop was loud and crisp, awakening the sleeping wolf in the cage just a few feet away.

"Sorry," Bruno said in the wolf's direction.

He didn't like the fact that Doctor Monk had taken the animal out of the forest. It looked so sad sitting there – almost like a dog in a kennel – that Bruno had considered opening the cage and letting the thing run right out of the van and into the forest. But the doctor was now paying both him and Charles double time-and-a-half around the clock, and the only way they were ever going to collect that money from the doctor was if they helped him get the wolf safely to the zoo in Vancouver. So as much as he wanted to help the wolf, he couldn't. There was just too much money at stake for him to do the right thing.

He pressed *play* and leaned back in his chair, waiting for an image to appear on the monitor. When he saw a sleeping wolf on the screen, he reached up and pressed *fast-forward*.

Lines suddenly appeared across the screen, slicing the image of the sleeping wolf into three equally distorted bands. Bruno watched the wolf twitch and jerk as it slept. And then, for a brief moment, the thing on the screen was no longer a wolf.

"What the –?"

Bruno stared at the screen for a few moments, and as he watched, the image changed from whatever it was, back to that of the sleeping wolf.

He stopped the machine, rewound the tape, and then pressed *play*, letting the image play out at its normal speed.

Again, there was the image of the sleeping wolf. A slight jerk of a paw, the wag of a tail, and the scratch of a hind leg at something itchy behind its left ear. And then . . .

"Whoa!"

The sleeping wolf on the screen changed shape, transforming into something that was halfway between a human and a wolf.

Bruno looked out the back of the van for Doctor Monk, but of course the man was inside the motel room. When he looked back at the screen, the image was of a wolf again. He rewound the tape and played it once more, this time making note of how long the thing spent transforming its shape.

No more than fifteen seconds, and most of that time was taken up by the transformation process itself. It couldn't have spent more than a few seconds in its hybrid form, but the duration of it really didn't matter, because all of it had been caught on tape.

Incredible! Bruno popped the tape from the machine and exited the van in search of Doctor Monk.

◆

"No way!" Michael Martin said in a hard, loud voice. Then his voice suddenly softened, and Noble could almost picture him crouching beside his bed with a hand over the receiver. "My father would kill me if he knew I was even thinking about doing something like that."

Noble had expected Michael to be hesitant, but he already sensed from the way Michael was talking that there were a few paths still open for Noble to convince him otherwise.

"It's really important that you do this," Noble said. "You know I wouldn't ask you if it weren't."

"Not only is it against the law, but I don't even think I could bring myself to do it. And if anyone found out I was the one who did it, my father would –" He cut himself off abruptly. "I don't even want to think about it."

"It's for Tora," Noble said, making a statement rather than pleading his case.

"What?"

"I said, it's for Tora."

"She's in trouble, isn't she?"

"Yes, she is."

"Big trouble?"

Noble was silent for the longest time. Finally, he said, "Her life depends on it."

Now it was Michael's turn to be silent.

"Are you still there?" asked Noble.

"All right," he sighed with just a hint of resignation in his voice. "When and where?"

Chapter 10

Doctor Monk stood in the middle of the motel room staring intently at the television, his eyes wide and unblinking.

Bruno's smile was ear-to-ear. "I told you it was good."

Monk didn't answer. Instead, he continued to stare at the screen until the transformation had gone full circle and the thing in the cage was a wolf once more.

"You like it, right?" Bruno asked, fishing for a compliment.

Again Monk didn't answer. He remained silent for several moments, then extended his hand toward the camera connected to the television and said, "Give me the tape!"

"Yeah, okay," said Bruno, offended by the abrupt nature

of the doctor's order. "I know the tape's yours. You made that clear before, remember."

Monk's expression softened, but just a bit. "No, it's not that. We have to get out of here as soon as possible."

"The man's coming from the ministry tonight," Charles reminded them. "We could be out of here first thing in the morning."

"No. We have to leave before that."

The two men just looked at the doctor, confused.

"Don't you realize what that thing in the cage is?" he said.

Bruno shrugged his shoulders.

Charles shook his head.

"It's a lycanthrope."

They both continued to look at him with blank stares.

"A werewolf!"

Bruno's jaw dropped and his eyes opened wide.

All the color seemed to be suddenly gone from Charles's face.

"Maybe the people around here know what it is, maybe they don't, but you can be sure of one thing. This . . . *creature* has got a few friends, and I doubt they're just going to stand around and watch us drive out of the forest with one of their kind caged up in the back of our truck."

Realization slowly dawned on Bruno and Charles. The looks of understanding on their faces quickly changed to masks of terror as they became aware of the danger they were in.

"I'll pack our bags," Bruno said.

"I'll get the van ready," said Charles.

Doctor Monk grabbed the tape, then glanced at his watch. "Late!" he spat, spinning on his heels and starting to pace the room. "Just what you'd expect from a damned government employee!"

Just then there was a knock at the door. Monk hurried over and pulled the door open. "What is it?"

"Doctor Edward Monk?"

"Yes."

"My name is Ethan Atherton."

Monk just looked at the man.

"I'm the damned government employee you've been waiting for."

•◆•

"I appreciate you coming so quickly," said Doctor Monk as he led Ethan Atherton out to the van. "It's important that we be on our way as soon as possible."

Atherton just looked at Monk.

"For the wolf's sake, of course," Monk added.

"Right," Atherton nodded. "I'm not quite clear on why the wolf has to be removed from the forest. Is it sick?"

Monk unlocked the back of the van and stood there without opening the door. "No, not at all. In fact, it's in perfect health."

"Then why do you have to take it anywhere? Can't you just tag it and study it in the wild?"

Monk pressed his lips together and slowly exhaled through his nostrils. Ethan Atherton was a wiry middle-aged man in his early to mid forties. He was well dressed in brown corduroy pants, a navy blue wool jacket, and a pair of heavy-duty hiking boots that looked like they'd just come out of the box. Looking at the man, Monk couldn't help thinking that Atherton was a city boy who was out of his element this far into the forest. But beneath his impeccable city clothes and freshly cut hair, there seemed to be an inner toughness to him. Monk got the impression that Atherton wasn't employed by the Ministry of the Environment by chance. He was likely a salad-eating tree-hugger who championed Mother Nature, and Monk made a note to be wary of him.

"Uh, that's just not possible," answered Monk.

"Why not?"

"It's a very unique animal. If we release it, we might not find another one like it."

"But if it's that rare, then it should be protected, no?"

Monk was running out of ideas. Realistically speaking, there was no reason that justified taking the animal out of the forest. Monk wanted the wolf out of the woods and in the controlled environment of a zoo so he could study the animal and begin preparing the television documentary that would make him rich and famous. It all sounded good, but somehow, Monk didn't think Atherton would think Monk's fame and fortune was a good enough reason to remove the wolf from its home. So, instead of arguing with the man, Monk decided to play his strong hand.

"Look, Mr. Atherton. I've been given permission to move this wolf to the zoo in Vancouver by your superiors. I suspect you have all the paperwork in your briefcase and all that's required for me to be on my way is a few signatures in the right places. If you don't wish me to make a call to the Minister, or the Premier, then I suggest you cut the small talk and give me what I need so I can get the hell out of here."

Atherton's eyes narrowed. Obviously he didn't like being talked to in such a manner.

"I've got the papers here," he said, gently patting his case, "but I have to be satisfied that the wolf is in good health before I release him to you. And judging by your attitude, Doctor Monk, I'm already getting the impression that the wolf is feeling poorly."

Touché, thought Monk. But he wasn't about to give the government man an inch.

He pulled open the door to the van and said, "The wolf has been under the care of a licensed veterinarian the whole time its been in my custody."

Atherton took a look around, cautiously making note of the conditions inside the van.

"You can stall all you wish, Mr. Atherton, but every minute of my time you waste brings me that much closer to making a phone call that could have a detrimental effect on your career."

Atherton glared at Monk for several tense moments. At one point, a soft cry from the wolf cut through the silence, causing the corners of Monk's lips to turn up in a smile.

Finally, without saying a single word, Atherton stepped inside the van.

Monk followed him in, closing the door behind them.

•◆•

Ranger Brock sat across the parking lot in his 4 x 4 as he watched the man from the Ministry of the Environment step into Doctor Monk's van. Just the sight of it turned the ranger's stomach. To think, someone was taking one of his children away from him and he was utterly powerless to do anything about it.

He shook his head and slammed a fist down onto the 4 x 4's dashboard. It was painfully obvious where he'd made his mistake. He'd believed that as long as he followed the rules, Tora would be protected. He had trusted that he and his fellow humans – all of them, as a race of people – would do the right thing and fight tooth and nail to maintain nature's balance.

He'd been let down, not by his friends or by any of the people in town, and not even by his immediate superiors in the Forest Service, but by their superiors, and by the people who lived and worked hundreds of miles away in glass and concrete towers. To them, Tora was just one of thousands of wolves in the province's forests. What was one more or one less wolf in the grand scheme of things?

Ranger Brock imagined the same thought being applied to the school in Redstone, which had hundreds of children within its walls. What if someone, a complete stranger, entered the school and walked the halls deciding to take one of the children away for research purposes? Who would miss that child? Only the people who loved it.

Ranger Brock lifted his cell phone from his duty belt and dialed the number of his home.

"Hello," Phyllis answered.

"Hi, Hon," he said.

"Is there any word?" she asked. "Have they come to their senses?"

Ranger Brock shook his head, almost forgetting to speak into the phone. "No," he said at last, "'fraid not."

"Oh, Garrett," she sighed.

The ranger could almost see the tears streaming down her face.

"Tell Noble that the man from the ministry is with Monk right now."

"Why? What does that mean?"

"It means that they'll be moving Tora soon."

"Okay, I'll tell him," she sniffed, then hung up without saying good-bye.

Ranger Brock closed his cell, replaced the phone on his belt, and got out of his 4 x 4.

Monk might have had permission to take Tora, but that didn't mean Ranger Brock was just going to let her go without a fight.

Chapter 11

The phone rang too many times for Noble's liking.

"Is he there?" Harlan asked.

Argus paced the floor, cracking his knuckles with each step.

Noble shook his head. "I don't understand it . . . he said he'd be home."

And then, as if on cue, the phone stopped ringing. "Hello?"

"Michael, where have you been?"

"Nowhere. Why?"

"You took so long to answer the phone."

"I was in the bathroom. It's still okay to go to the bathroom isn't it?"

"Yes, of course."

"What is it?"

"It's time."

"Time for what?"

Noble hesitated. This was no time for Michael Martin to have a change of heart. "For you to do the thing we talked about before."

"You mean I have to do it?"

"Yes, you've already agreed to it."

"I know, but I was hoping . . . you know, that it would all work out on its own somehow."

"Well, it hasn't."

Michael sighed.

"Can we count on you?"

Silence.

"Can *Tora* count on you?"

"Yeah, okay," he said at last. "I'll do it."

Noble said just two words. "Thank you."

◆

Monk and the man from the ministry were still inside the van by the time Ranger Brock reached it. The rear door was unlocked, and he could hear the two of them talking.

"As you can see, the wolf has not been harmed in any way," Monk was saying.

"I don't know. It's hard to tell such a thing when the animal is in a cage."

Ranger Brock smiled. It was obvious the man from the ministry was on Tora's side. The ranger couldn't be sure, but it sounded as if he were trying to convince the doctor to open up the cage. Once that happened, Tora would surely try to escape, bounding out of the trailer where nary a soul would lift a finger to stop her.

But Monk was having none of it.

"This animal isn't getting out of this cage until we reach the zoo in Vancouver. Now, I've been patient with you Mr. Atherton, but all you've been doing is stalling. I have the legal right to move this animal . . . and you've got papers that say as much in that briefcase of yours. Either you sign the papers and let me leave within the next ten minutes, or I start making a new round of phone calls designed to make your life rather miserable."

"Is that a threat?"

"As a matter of fact, it is."

Ranger Brock could hear them moving toward him, exiting the van. He stepped back and opened the door for them.

"Ah, Ranger Brock," said Doctor Monk, stepping down from the van. "Just in time to see Mr. Atherton hand over the papers that will make this legal."

Ranger Brock crossed his arms over his chest and said, "I don't care what those papers say. I'm not letting you leave here with that wolf."

"Really?" Doctor Monk smiled, unconcerned. "How dramatic."

•◆•

"All right, let's go," said Noble.

The three brothers had left their clothes behind in their bedrooms and were ready for the trip to the Redstone Inn.

"You sure we're doing the right thing here?" asked Harlan.

"It'll be dangerous, Harlan, maybe one of us will get hurt . . . or worse," said Noble. "If you want to stay here until we come back, I won't hold it against you."

Harlan seemed to consider the offer.

Argus looked at Harlan as if he might be crazy. "They're taking your sister to a zoo," he said, giving him a slap on the shoulder.

Harlan nodded. "Right. Sorry."

Noble put a hand on Harlan's other shoulder. "It's better that we do this together."

"I'm with you."

"I know."

Noble opened the bedroom door and looked down the hallway. It wasn't as if Phyllis would stop them from going on a run through the forest, but if she saw them she might ask questions about where they were going and how long they'd be. They could lie to her, but she'd always been able to tell whenever they weren't telling the truth. And, since Tora had been caught while out on a run, it was possible that Phyllis might ask them to stay home today. It was better for everyone just to avoid the confrontation all together.

There was no one around. The house was silent.

The three brothers padded down the hallway to the sliding kitchen door that opened up to the forest.

Noble opened the door and held it for Argus and Harlan. When they were out of the house, he closed the door silently, then followed his two brothers across the lawn toward the trees roughly thirty yards from the house.

But instead of waiting until they were in the forest to transform, Argus began his change on the run. It was something they had practiced a few times before, but never with as much urgency as now.

Argus leaned forward, his arms pumping furiously as he ran. As his left arm arced forward, it was human, but as it came back, it was lupine. The arm was large, muscular, and hairy, not quite fully transformed into the finely sculpted forepaw of a wolf, but well on its way to getting there. His legs experienced a similar transformation. One moment they were human, another moment they were wolflike: short, muscular, and covered with a coat of fine gray hair. The entire transformation took less than six strides to complete, the first stride made on two legs and the sixth made on four.

Noble completed his own transformation just as quickly, surprised that the change had felt so natural. As he glanced ahead, he saw Argus bound into the forest with a huge leap over a seedling. Harlan was several strides behind, apparently having some trouble completing his transformation on the run, judging by the patches of skin about his body that remained bare. Noble hurried forward, nipping at Harlan's hind legs to help Harlan's transformation and to help speed him on his way. Harlan raced away from Noble's bites and by the time he reached the forest he was fully covered in a thick coat of silver-gray fur.

Noble followed his brothers into the forest. The earth felt good beneath his paws, and the smell of the forest seemed to charge him with enormous energy, driving him and his brothers forward harder and faster than they'd ever run before in their lives.

The run was exhilarating, no question about it. But Noble knew that however good this felt, it would pale in comparison to the leisurely walk they would be making on their return home . . . with Tora leading the way.

•—•

"Boys?"

Phyllis came up the stairs from the basement, where she'd been doing some laundry to help keep her mind off of Tora's desperate situation. She'd heard the kitchen door slide open and shut, and now the boys weren't answering her.

She went into the kitchen and looked out across the yard toward the line of trees behind the house.

A sapling twitched at the edge of the forest, but other than that, there was no sign of the boys anywhere.

"Good luck," she muttered under her breath.

Chapter 12

"I can't let you leave with the wolf," said Ranger Brock, confronting Doctor Monk as the man left his motel room. His two assistants were standing at either side of the van. Inside it, Tora was growling softly as the two men spoke.

"Why not?" Monk replied, looking the Ranger in the eye. "I have permission from every conceivable level of government and organization with any authority over the matter . . . including the one you belong to."

"I don't care. It's wrong."

"Is it?" Monk said, his voice rising in tone. "Or is there something else at stake."

Monk closed the distance between himself and Ranger Brock, looking at him more closely, eyeing him as if he were looking for a speck of dust on his uniform.

"What do you know about the wolf?"

"It belongs in the forest."

"Yes, yes, of course it does, but what *else* do you know about it?"

Although he tried desperately to steel himself against it, Ranger Brock felt himself twitch. "It's a magnificent creature, and you have no right to take it from its home."

"Ah, its home. Where might that be? The forest, yes, but what about when it's not in the forest. A house, perhaps. Maybe a house in the forest where the call of the wild is always just a few steps away. That would be a perfect place for such a creature."

"What are you talking about?"

"Oh, I think you know very well what I'm talking about." Monk started to circle the ranger. Then he stopped and smiled. "How is it that I – someone from the city who scarcely knows his way around a redwood – was able to recognize something different about this wolf after two days filming, and you – a forest ranger who has spent most of his life in these woods, knows nothing of what I am talking about?"

Bruno and Charles, still waiting for the doctor on either side of the van, snickered.

"So, I've either stumbled across something that you've never ever seen before, or you're lying to protect some secret that you desperately want to preserve."

"That's ridiculous," Ranger Brock said, feeling himself going on the defensive as Monk slowly gained the upper hand.

"Are there more wolves like this one out there?" Monk asked.

"There are hundreds, maybe even thousands of wolves like it."

"I don't think so." Monk paused for a moment, then said, "You've got four children, haven't you?"

"What's that got to do with anything?"

Monk shrugged. "Nothing, I suppose. Except that I hear the four of them are all the same age, but none of them are twins."

"So?"

Inside the van Tora began to growl with more fury.

Monk ignored her. "And they're not your biological children, are they?"

"We adopted them."

"That was very kind of you and your wife . . . four children at once."

"We didn't even have to discuss it."

"Of course not, you both realized how unique they were."

"Every child is special in its way."

Monk laughed. "I wonder how many of your children were at school today."

"All of them."

"Are you sure? Or perhaps only three made it there for attendance this morning."

Ranger Brock said nothing, wondering if Monk was bluffing or he'd actually called the school.

"Are they all like this one?" Monk asked, leaving the school question behind.

"They're all great kids."

"Because if they are like this one, I'll be back. And so will hundreds of biologists, anthropologists, geneticists, hell, there'll even be reporters here from newspapers like *The Weekly World News.*

Ranger Brock had had enough. "You're not going to get away with this. I won't allow it."

Tora howled, pacing her cage.

Monk just laughed and said, "I've already gotten away with it." He raised his right hand to show Brock the papers he held in his tight little fist. "Now step aside."

"I won't," said the ranger.

"What are you going to do? Hit me? Pummel me? Beat me until I let the wolf go?"

More noise from inside the van.

"If that's what it takes."

Monk just sighed.

"You won't do anything of the sort," said a voice.

Ranger Brock turned to see Sergeant Martin standing off to the side.

"What?"

"I'm sorry, Garrett," said the sergeant.

"You can't just let him leave with her . . ."

"I received very specific instructions from my inspector. He wants me to escort the doctor . . ." He lowered his eyes. "and the wolf, out of Redstone without any trouble."

Tora began to moan softly. It was obvious that she'd heard the conversation and realized that one of her last chances for freedom was lost and her fate had been decided once and for all.

"What are you going to do if I don't cooperate?" said the ranger. "Put me in jail?"

The sergeant let out a sigh, and said, "If I have to."

Monk's smile was ear-to-ear. "Now step aside," he said. "The sooner I'm out of this place, the better."

Ranger Brock took a step to the left to let Monk by, avoiding the man's gaze in case a tear for Tora had leaked from the corner of his eye.

Monk stepped inside the van while his two men jumped into the front cab, ready to leave.

Sergeant Martin stepped in front of Ranger Brock and put a hand on the ranger's shoulder. "I don't like it any more than you do," he said. "But I have my orders."

Ranger Brock nodded, but said nothing.

·••·

Michael Martin made his way through the forest, pushing aside branches and leaping over seedlings and brush. His heart was pumping inside his chest like the bass drum of the school's marching band, but it wasn't from the effort he was putting out traveling the forest. He could feel his heart *thumping, thumping, thumping*, as if it might explode, but he couldn't do anything to stop it or slow it down. Not stop and rest, not breathe deeply. Nothing at all. What they wanted him to do was wrong, against the law. Even worse was if his father ever found out what he did, his life would be over. Over. Over and out. Over and done with.

But what about Tora?

The guys were vague about what had happened to her, but from what he could gather, she was in trouble. Not out-past-curfew trouble, but really serious her-life-hangs-in-the-balance kind of trouble.

Michael shook his head. How does a teenage girl get into life-hangs-in-the-balance kind of trouble, anyway? He knew the answer to the question before he even finished asking it. Tora wasn't just a teenage girl, and her three brothers weren't just teenage boys. Michael didn't quite know exactly what was so different about the four of them, but they were *different*, that was for sure.

They liked him well enough, but they didn't mix all that well with the rest of the kids at school. And they were secretive too, as if there was something about them that would be disastrous to them all if anyone ever learned what it was.

And then there was the rage. It wasn't so evident with Tora and Harlan, maybe not even with Noble, but Argus sure had it in spades. The guy always seemed to be seething under his skin, as if he were constantly *this close* to snapping and letting this inhuman anger bubble to the surface. No wonder kids stayed away from them. Who wanted to risk making an enemy out of Argus Brock? You might as well hold a rattlesnake to your neck and bet on whether it might bite if you pull on its tail.

Michael crested a hill and could see a sparse patch of land sloping away from him. To the west, he could see the still blue waters of Puntzi Lake, while to the east, he could hear the rushing waters of the Chilcotin River.

There was water on two sides of the land and a road, with easy access, to the south. That made the spot just about perfect for his purposes.

He headed toward the road, still thinking. He'd had his suspicions about the four Brock kids for years, but he'd never been able to figure out just what they were all about. His first inclination had been that they'd all been abused as children and Ranger Brock had rescued them from a certain life of misery. But after a while he realized that they were all too self-confident for that to be the case. He thought they might have been abandoned in the wild, but they seemed to love the forest too much for that to be true. Perhaps they'd been the children of some mountain couple, who left them on the ranger's doorstep when life got too tough to support so many children.

Plausible explanations all of them, but none was a perfect fit. They were strong and smart and loved to laugh and have fun. They were at home in the forest and were always wary of people, no matter how good their intentions. It was as if they were outsiders and always would be, no matter how much people accepted them or treated them with kindness.

Michael was a prime example of that. He was probably their best friend in the whole world, yet he could stuff everything he knew about them inside a shoe box and still have room for a size ten pair of Nikes. And still, they asked him to do this, and he'd agreed.

"I must be crazy," he said.

He stopped a moment in the middle of a fairly dense patch of brush. *This will do nicely*, he thought, slipping the knapsack off his back. He breathed one last sigh, then zipped open the pack and began taking out what he needed.

With water so close by and easy access to the road, putting out a fire here wouldn't be too difficult to do. If things happened to get out of control, a fire might burn for a little while before anyone could get here, but once the wardens and forest rangers arrived on the scene, they'd probably be able to get things under control in no time flat.

At least he hoped that would be the case. It was always possible for the wind to pick up, or turn, and have a whole mountainside go up in flames. Well, it was a risk he'd have to take.

Michael was convinced Tora's life was at stake, and if Noble asked him to help by starting a fire outside of Redstone, then that's what he would do.

Michael squeezed out a stream of lighter fluid into the heart of the brush and let it soak into the leaves and branches. Then he spent the next twenty minutes gathering up leaves and wood, both dried and freshly green, and piled it all up next to the brush. When he had a pile that would last him a half-hour or so, he took out the lighter fluid once more and drew a line of fluid on the ground so he could light it a safe distance away from the brush.

He took a deep breath and held it a moment as he slid his knapsack back onto his shoulders.

"I sure hope this works," he said.

He pulled a book of matches from the Redstone Inn from his pocket, opened the cover, and tore a match stick from the row inside it. He drew the match against the flint strip at the back of the book, but the match head crumbled under the pressure. He opened the book again and tore out another match. This one lit, but by the time he got it to the ground, the movements of his shaking hand had blown the flaming match out.

He took a moment to compose himself, then tried it again. This time the match flared without incident. He lowered the burning head down toward the damp line of earth leading away from the brush. Closer. Closer.

When the match touched the ground, the flame jumped, doubling in height. Then it crept along the ground toward the bush where – *Whumpf!*

The brush exploded into flame.

It was all fairly dry so everything burned cleanly. Michael piled a few long-dead branches onto the burning bush to ensure the fire would burn hot and with plenty of flames.

Finally, when he had a roaring fire going in the middle of the slight clearing, he picked up one of the green branches he'd scavenged and laid it over the fire.

Nothing happened for a few moments, but then the green leaves began to smoke. A big plume of dirty white smoke lingered over the fire, and then the leaves slowly began to curl from the heat and flame.

Thick white smoke rose up from the fire.

He tossed another branch onto it, this one from a spruce tree. The needles on it were bright green and sizzled when they came in contact with the flame. The new branch nearly smothered the fire, creating a thick stream of even heavier white smoke. The smoke wafted lazily up from the fire, growing into a larger and larger plume with each foot it rose up from the ground.

Michael put another branch on the fire, then another, and another. In no time at all there was a streak of smoke rising up through the trees. There was plenty of smoke, but was it enough to fool someone into thinking the forest was on fire?

Michael kept working the fire, fanning the flames, and sending more and more smoke billowing into the air. He was in a tricky spot. He had to make sure the fire was smoking well enough to draw people's attention, but he couldn't hang around so long that they'd find him at the scene.

He looked overhead and saw the smoke thinning as it broke clear of the trees. He needed to do more. He reached into his knapsack and took out three lengths of black PVC pipe, the kind plumbers used for household drains. He tossed them onto the fire and suddenly, black smoke rose dramatically into the sky in a great dark cloud.

There, Michael thought. *I've done it.*

He watched the fire smoke and smolder for another few minutes. When the smoke had risen some forty or fifty yards into the air, he checked one last time to make sure the fire wouldn't spread, then he turned and ran . . .

Like the wind.

Chapter 13

Argus was the first to arrive at the Redstone Inn a short time later. Noble was seconds behind him, while Harlan brought up the rear less than a minute later.

The van was still parked in the lot, but there seemed to be plenty of activity going on around it. There were several RCMP cruisers in the lot, two of them parked at the entrance, while Ranger Brock's 4 x 4 was still in the same spot it had been in the night before.

Noble sniffed the air but could smell nothing out of the ordinary. Then he listened and heard Tora snarling inside the van. Noble looked to his left and realized that Argus had heard Tora as well. The big gray wolf was bouncing up and down on his front paws, agitated and likely wanting to bound across the lot, break into the back of the van, and tear Tora out of her cage.

Noble couldn't let that happen. It would have been a fine plan yesterday, when no one had been around, but today there would be too many witnesses to such an escape. What sort of reaction would people have to three wolves acting precisely and in unison to rescue one of their own? What kind of attention would wolves with the intelligence of humans bring to the forest they lived in? The stories would spread quickly. Before long, there would be people wandering the woods in search of intelligent wolves, or claiming to have run or even danced with the wolves of the Redstone Forest. The wolf pack would become the equivalent of the Bigfoot myth, and there would be more cameras amongst the trees than people in town. That would never do.

Noble rose up on his hind legs, opened his maw, and bit into the thick fur along Argus's neck. The move caught the bigger wolf off guard and he fell to the ground hard.

Argus voiced his disapproval by chuffing at Noble, but did nothing more to challenge his wishes. He got up and stared at the van, his gaze unwavering and his eyes unblinking.

Noble resumed his observation of the lot, and, judging by the amount of movement, it looked as if Monk and his men were making preparations to leave. Noble took a look at the shadows cast by the men in the parking lot. There couldn't be more than an hour of sunlight left to the day.

Monk would be gone before sundown, but he wouldn't be out of the forest until well after dark. That suited Noble just fine. A hint of a smile appeared on his maw. Now, if only Michael Martin would come through with his end of the plan.

•─◆─•

Sergeant Martin's cruiser was positioned in front of Doctor Monk's van but was stationary. Another RCMP cruiser was positioned behind the van and it too was parked.

Bruno was behind the wheel of the van with Charles in the passenger seat. Doctor Monk had been in the back of the truck, but after several minutes' delay he'd come out to see what the hold up was.

"What are we waiting for?" Monk said, heading toward Sergeant Martin's cruiser. "Let's go, already."

The sergeant rolled down his window and said, "There's something going on."

"What?"

"Don't know yet. We've been advised to stand by for further instructions."

Doctor Monk threw his hands in the air, then slapped them down hard against the sides of his legs. "Can't you people do anything quickly?"

"Look, Doctor. I've been *ordered* to help you. That's not the same as *wanting* to help you. I'm not exactly in any hurry to help you steal an animal from this forest."

"Your supervisor will be hearing about this!"

The sergeant nodded. "Don't trouble yourself. It'll all be in my report."

Doctor Monk was about to turn and stomp away when the radio inside Sergeant Martin's cruiser crackled.

"We've received a report of a forest fire that's just started west of Puntzi Lake between the lake and the Chilcotin River," the calm, soft-spoken female voice said. "Fire crews have been dispatched. All available units are asked to assist with road access and preparation for the possible evacuation of residents on the outskirts of Redstone."

Sergeant Martin shook his head.

"What is it?" Monk asked.

"Your lucky day, doctor."

Monk seemed confused.

"We've just been called out to a forest fire," the sergeant smiled.

"Meaning?"

"Meaning, you're on your own."

"So I can leave, then?"

"Any time you like."

Monk hesitated a moment, then finally said, "Okay, great. I'll be on my way then."

◆

Ranger Brock closed his cell phone and clenched the device tightly in his fist. *Of all the times to be called away on a fire*, he thought. *Just as Monk is about to leave with Tora.*

The ranger stared through the windshield of his 4 x 4 watching Sergeant Martin's cruiser leave the parking lot and head north toward the fire.

He must have just gotten the call as well . . . leaving Monk to make the trip into Vancouver on his own.

Initially it had seemed like some of the worst luck imaginable, but as he watched the second RCMP cruiser leave the lot, the ranger realized that every emergency service personnel within twelve miles had probably been called to the fire.

RCMP.

Firefighters.

Forest rangers.

Anyone with any kind of authority.

Which meant if anything happened to Doctor Monk and his men on their way toward the main highway, it might be some time before any sort of help could get to them. Ranger Brock thought about that for a few moments and a slight smile slowly broke across his face.

The area where the fire was burning was easily accessible by road. There was a lake and a river nearby that pumpers could access, and old logging roads in the area would serve as breaks if the fire got out of control. Basically it was a fire that wasn't going to last very long. Only long enough to grab everyone's attention for a little while and distract them from everything else that was happening around town – like Doctor Monk's theft of Tora.

The ranger's smile grew larger. He had a feeling that the boys were at the bottom of this. While he could never approve of them deliberately setting fire to the forest, he had to admire their ingenuity.

Ranger Brock put the 4 x 4 in gear and drove up alongside Monk's van in time to catch the doctor climbing into the back of it. "Drive carefully, doctor," he said. "The roads around here can sometimes be very treacherous – and full of danger."

Monk nodded and forced a smile.

As Ranger Brock drove away, he couldn't help notice that there was a subtle hint of fear on the doctor's face. The ranger thought it looked good on him.

Chapter 14

The three wolves watched the parking lot with unwavering gazes. Something was happening, but they couldn't be sure what. People were running. Cars had begun to move. Sergeant Martin's cruiser and the other RCMP vehicles were leaving the parking lot, turning north, and driving off in a hurry.

Maybe Michael Martin has done it, thought Noble. It sure looked that way.

To Noble's left, Harlan sniffed the air a few times then gave a little yelp. Even though Noble couldn't smell it himself, Harlan had detected the scent of Michael's fire on the air. It would have to be a decent-sized fire for them to be able to smell it this far away, and so soon. But then again, Harlan could smell a rabbit over a hundred yards away, and smoke had been easy for him to detect ever since they'd been pups.

At last Ranger Brock's 4 x 4 rolled forward. There could be no doubt now. Michael had done it. The fire was burning, and the game was on.

Ranger Brock pulled to a stop next to Monk's van just as Monk was climbing into the back of it. He remained stationary a few moments, then left the lot, turning north like the others.

Monk's van remained parked in the lot for more than a minute.

To Noble's right, Argus seemed agitated. It was obvious that he wanted to race across the parking lot, incapacitate the van, and rip the humans from inside it one by one.

Noble leaned to his right, rubbing shoulders with Argus in an attempt to calm him down. Argus growled low and throaty but did not move. Noble was pleased. They had a plan that needed to be followed. The last thing they needed, Tora especially, was to do something impulsive. Monk would be getting what he deserved – when the time was right.

◆◆◆

Michael Martin walked casually along the shoulder of the old dirt logging road that hugged the southern shore of the Chilcotin River. There was a cabin about a quarter mile down river. If he didn't hear anything by the time he reached it, Michael would knock on the door and ask the people inside to call or radio for help. But he doubted he'd need to do that.

Even walking on this road, with trees reaching forty and fifty feet toward the sky on either side of him, he could still see the gray smoke hanging over the tops of the trees. If he could see it from the ground, surely the ranger manning the watchtower along the Nechako Range could see it too.

Michael kicked at a stone lying in the road and watched as it tumbled and flipped down the center of the roadway then turned sharply right wheeling off the road into the ditch. He was about to kick at another stone when he heard something in the forest. It was mechanical, constant, and growing louder.

He stopped in his tracks and listened more closely. Vehicles. Small ones leading the way, followed by larger ones. Police and fire crews.

Michael looked left and right. There was a shallow ditch on either side of the road, but neither of them were deep enough to hide in. He looked again to his left, toward the river. Nowhere to hide there. He looked right. There was a gently rising slope covered with trees. The trees were spaced widely enough that he could see clearly for a distance of about fifty yards. There was no way he'd be able to run that far before the trucks arrived. But he had to hide, somehow, somewhere. How would it look if the sergeant's son was the only person in an area where a fire had been deliberately set – with a pack of matches in his pocket, a can of lighter fluid in his knapsack, reeking of fresh smoke, and with a thick dusting of ash in his hair?

The vehicles were getting closer. Louder.

Michael dashed into the forest and up the slope, running as fast as his legs would carry him.

The trucks were almost upon him.

He had to hide somewhere. Anywhere.

He dove behind a tree, rolled onto the ground, and did his best to cover his body with humus. It stank of rotten wood and leaves, and it felt wet and slimy against the skin of his neck and face. But it was hiding him. Camouflage. He grabbed great handfuls of the stuff and threw it all over his body. He could feel wet leaves and tiny sticks getting jammed into his shoes, under his shirt, and down his pants . . . as he became one with the nature around him.

The trucks were just to his left. They were passing him now, traveling at a good clip.

He stilled his body, held his breath, and waited. Surely no one was looking into the forest for a teenager wearing an earthen disguise.

Eventually, the roar of the trucks faded. He could hear them slowing farther down the road as they neared the site of the fire.

At last, Michael began to breathe again. He opened his eyes, lifted his head, and found himself face to face with a lynx, a wild cat about the size of the family dog. Michael gasped and once again held his breath.

The lynx stared at him with wide eyes and pricked ears, seemingly startled to see something rising up out of the ground. In fact, it appeared to be as afraid of Michael as Michael was of it.

"Hey there," Michael said weakly, slowly getting up onto his hands and knees.

The big cat's back went up in an arch as it turned to the side and awkwardly backed away from him. It stood like that for several seconds, straining to make itself as big as possible.

"How's it goin'?" he said, his voice gaining a bit of strength.

The big cat twitched once, then turned and ran as fast as its huge padded feet could carry it.

"'Fraidy cat!" Michael laughed.

Seconds later the lynx was gone. Michael got up onto his feet, brushed himself off, and continued on his way.

The road out of Redstone was a twisted ribbon of dirt that wended its way through the trees and around the mountains. While it was twelve miles to the main highway by car, it was closer to ten on foot – which suited the pack's purposes nicely.

When Monk's van exited the parking lot of the Redstone Inn, it turned right, heading north. While the pack headed south.

Just a few miles away, the road turned and doubled back on itself, making vehicles travel an extra mile, and giving the pack – which would be cutting through the forest – plenty of time to get ahead of the van and be ready for it when they crossed paths.

They'd chosen a stretch of road about midway between Redstone and the main highway because that section of it was narrow and lined by thick stands of trees on either side. The height of the forest blocked out much of the sun, and now, still an hour before sunset, the forest was already dark and covered by a net of long tangled shadows.

On the west side of the road, the land sloped upward at a sharp angle, providing an excellent vantage point from which to watch traffic on the road as well as offering the brothers a position of strength, which would come in handy once the van had been stopped. On the east side of the road, the slope continued its descent where it eventually was intersected by another section of roadway. The distance between the roads was less than twenty yards but it might as well have been twenty miles due to the angle of the slope and the number of trees standing guard. Anyone running down that slope risked a fall, which meant rolling the rest of the way, bounding over every bump, and bouncing off every tree. In short, it was a perfect place to stop someone and to keep them from getting away.

The three wolves arrived by the side of the road less than ten minutes after leaving the Redstone Inn. But time was still short since Monk's van was on its way, and this time it would take several minutes for all three of them to undergo the change.

Noble, as leader, went first. He found a redwood that was as thick around as a mailbox and let out a howl to let the others know what he was about to do. Then he rose up on his hind legs and placed his forepaws as high up on the trunk as he could manage. Stretched out against the tree, Noble was over five feet long in his wolfen form, and he'd be extending that length considerably by the time he was through.

His paws were the first to begin changing shape, fingers lengthening and curling, claws darkening until they were as black as the forest floor. Then his bones began to grow, expanding in all directions. At the same time, his muscles grew larger as well, stretching taut against the pull of his bones, then bulking up to fill out his expanded frame.

And while Noble's body was growing internally, his flesh was growing to accommodate the change. As hair sprouted thick and gray all over his expanding body, the skin beneath it itched as if it were crawling with spiders. It was an uncomfortable feeling, one that he'd never experienced over every part of his body. But it was a small price to pay for Tora's life.

Changing shape from human form to that of the wolf had almost become routine for the pack, but it was quite tricky for them to take the shape of something in between the two forms. Humans and wolves were both natural beings, occupying their own place in the Earth Mother's grand scheme of things. But the werewolf was neither human nor wolf. There was no place for the creature in the natural world and as such it existed outside the realm of nature. Werewolves were uncommon, unusual, otherworldly, extraordinary, supernatural.

Eventually, the uncomfortable itch of his skin and the pain in his bones began to fade, and Noble's body surged with an inhuman strength. A feeling of power seemed to flow through his body like an electric current.

Now he stood over six feet tall and weighed well over two hundred pounds. His arms were longer, almost apelike. He had his hands again, which he could use to grab and hold, squeeze and tear, but the extra length allowed him to run on all fours if he had to. His teeth had lengthened too, sharpening into fearsome fangs. And the claws at the ends of his fingers had become deadly, knife-edged talons. And as a testament to his half-man half-wolf form, he'd retained a short length of silver-gray tail that would help him keep his balance on the run.

Noble flexed his arms, feeling the strength and power of his muscles. They had undergone the change many times before, but never for any purpose. It had always been simply for practice, a training exercise so they'd be ready if and when they needed their werewolf form. Ranger Brock had warned them about the form, explaining that possessing such power could be dangerous. Noble had never understood why the ranger had been so cautious about it, but it made sense to him now. He felt strong, powerful, almost invincible, and there was a distinct feeling of anger and aggression coursing through his veins. If he let his emotions get away from him, even for a moment, he could end up tearing Monk and his men apart just as easily as he might kill a fly.

It was a dangerous ability to have and it scared Noble a little. He hoped Argus and Harlan felt the same way, because fearing what they could do with their bodies might prevent them from abusing their power.

With that thought still on his mind, Noble looked behind him and saw that both Argus and Harlan were nearing the end of their transformation as well. Harlan was now nearly six feet tall, while Argus had shot up to well over seven. That was a dramatic enough change, but it was their faces that amazed Noble.

They had become something between man and wolf. Their faces were covered with fur, with wolflike snouts and lips that could easily be pulled back to reveal rows of glistening, menacing fangs. Their ears had become triangular and pointed, able to move forward and back to help locate things with a heightened sense of hearing. But for all the changes they'd undergone, they still retained all the features of their human faces. Anyone looking at them, even in this most unnatural form, would recognize the childlike innocence of Harlan, and Argus's stoic square jaw. And the two distinct colors of his eyes made Argus even more fearsome. Overall, it was as if they had taken the best of each species and made something that was better than both of them.

Argus stretched his full length and drew his claws back against the trunk of the tree he rested against. Eight fresh gouges appeared in the wood, each one a full quarter-inch deep.

Harlan tried the same move against a nearby tree and managed to only make eight faint scratches in the bark.

Argus howled at his little brother, then tussled the unmistakable thatch of black hair atop Harlan's head.

Noble stepped away from the other two, then stretched and flexed his muscles until he was sure that the change was complete.

"Ready?" Noble said, his voice deep, throaty, and rough.

"Been ready for a while," Argus said, flexing his clawlike hands, his voice sounding as if it had originated in some deep dark cavern.

"Me too!" Harlan said. His voice was nowhere near as fearsome as the others', but no one chided him about it. Although smaller than Noble and Argus, he would still be a force for any human to reckon with.

"Then let's get our sister back."

Without another word, the three werewolves set to work.

Chapter 15

"Uh, oh," Bruno said.

"What is it?" asked Charles.

"Look!"

"Uh, oh."

Bruno took his foot off the accelerator.

The door between the cab and the back of the van slid open. Doctor Monk stuck his head through the opening and said, "Why are we slowing down?"

Bruno lifted his head in the direction of the road before them. "There's a tree down across the road."

"Can't you go around it?" Monk asked.

"If this thing had wings, maybe."

"Make sure you lock the doors when you get out to move it."

Bruno looked at Charles. Both of them had a puzzled expression on their faces.

"You want us to get out of the van?" asked Bruno.

"It's dark out there, you know."

"How else are we going to get by?" Monk said.

Bruno brought the van to a stop. The headlight beams momentarily dipped down onto the road, then rose up to illuminate the fallen tree. "I don't know. I thought maybe we could turn around and go back."

"Go back!" Monk spat. "Are you out of your mind? We're not going back to that two-bit town. Not tonight, not ever."

"Okay," Bruno nodded. "It's just that I don't think that tree is there by accident, you know. Maybe somebody put it there to make us stop."

Monk hesitated a moment, then said, "Nonsense! We've got permission to leave and everything's in order. Take a look around, for crying out loud! We're in the forest. Trees fall down all the time. Now get out there and move it out of the way. We've already wasted enough time talking about it."

Monk punctuated his order by slamming the sliding door closed.

"Why don't you come outside and help us, Doctor Monk?" Charles muttered under his breath.

"Because someone has to stay inside the truck and look after the wolf," came the muffled response from the back of the van.

Bruno and Charles just looked at each other, shaking their heads.

"Should we go?" Bruno asked.

Charles nodded reluctantly. "The tree's not going to move itself."

"Would be neat if it did, though."

"Yeah, that would be a trick."

A pause.

"You have a flashlight?"

"I think so, let me check the batteries."

Charles reached down between his legs and produced a sturdy green flashlight that was black at both ends. He switched it on and shone its beam out through the front windshield at the tree.

"Hey, that works nice," Bruno said.

"Doesn't it though?"

"Would you two quit stalling and get out there!" Monk shouted from the back of the van.

"I guess we gotta go," Bruno said with a shrug.

Charles nodded. "Who wants to live for ever anyway?"

"You first."

"After you."

"Get going!" Monk shouted.

Bruno sighed.

Charles zipped up his jacket.

The two men finally got out of the van.

•◆•

Bruno Buono was scared. Sure, he'd been scared plenty of times before in his life, but not like this. This was unreal.

The woods were dark. No, more than just dark, they were black with only a hint of light coming from the sliver of moon overhead. Without the headlights shining out from the front of the van, they'd be lost. And on top of all that, the forest seemed alive somehow. In the city, when you turned down a dark alley, there was always a chance you might run into some trouble. A *chance* of trouble. Here, Bruno knew, there wasn't a chance of finding trouble, it was guaranteed he would find it.

After all, Doctor Monk had trapped the wolf, held it hostage, and then stolen it from the forest. Sure, Monk had managed to get all the paperwork that made it legal, but somehow Bruno didn't think the creatures in this forest gave a damn about that. The governments of British Columbia and Canada didn't hold a candle to the laws of Mother Nature, and all of Monk's powerful friends and legal documents didn't amount to anything at the moment.

They were three men, three *city* men in the middle of the forest, who could barely see the ground in front of them, while creatures that could change their shape from wolf to human and who knows what else were creeping through the woods all around them. Bruno couldn't see them, but he knew they were there.

"We're screwed," he said.

Charles, who Bruno could hardly see even though the man was no more than six feet to his right, said, "That tree's not that big. We should be able to get it out of the way, no problem."

"I'm not talking about the tree."

"Then what?"

"You think that tree just happened to fall across the road today?"

"You're saying someone put it there?"

"That's right."

"Who?"

"Who do you think?"

Charles was silent for several seconds, then said, "We *are* screwed."

Just then, the headlights of the van winked out behind them and the two men found themselves in total darkness.

"Uh oh," Charles said.

"Let's get back to the van."

Bruno turned and ran – slamming head first into a wall of muscle and fur. The force of the impact sent him reeling backward and he fell to the ground, landing hard on his rear end and hitting the back of his head against the roadway. Bright spikes of pain flashed behind his eyes and he let out a groan. He rose up onto his elbows and rubbed the back of his head with his right hand. There was a huge bump there, but luckily the skin hadn't been broken.

He stayed on the ground, listening to the sounds of the forest. In addition to the chittering of bugs, the rustling of leaves, and the occasional hooting of an owl, he could hear Charles's footsteps fading into the distance.

And there was another sound too, one that Bruno couldn't explain. It sounded like heavy breathing. Heavy breathing out in the middle of the forest.

Bruno dreaded opening his eyes but knew there was no way around it. He had to open them, had to see for himself what the hell it was that he'd run into. He hoped it had been a furry brick wall, since that's what it had felt like, but he knew it was probably something much, much worse.

Slowly, he opened his right eye. Then his left. His eyes had adjusted some to the darkness now and he could make out things more clearly than he could just a few minutes before. Still, being able to see didn't help his situation any.

What he saw was an absolutely magnificent creature in front of him standing well over seven feet tall, its body a mass of rippling muscle and silver-gray fur. Its hands were made up of five beefy fingers and tipped with claws as sharp as knife blades. Its head was large and rounded at the back and capped by a pair of triangular-shaped ears. The front of the head protruded in a long snout, the lips of which were pulled back to reveal rows of razor-sharp teeth that looked powerful enough to snap off an arm with a single bite. And the eyes, they were two different colors. One green, one blue. And whether it was a trick of the moonlight or a product of the fear he felt, Bruno couldn't be sure, but the thing's eyes seemed to glow with an anger and fury that burned somewhere deep down inside it.

There was no doubt in Bruno's mind that the creature intended to kill him – kill him slowly and with as much pain and suffering as possible.

Bruno wanted to get up and run, run as fast as he could, but his body was not responding. He was frozen in place, unable to move more than a few inches before the grip of fear held him firmly in place. In the end, all he could do was cower like some frightened child in the formidable presence of an awesome beast.

Bruno took a moment to consider his life and how there were several loose ends that he wished he'd taken care of. He owed the government some back taxes, his apartment was an absolute mess, and he'd never asked his long-time girlfriend, Florence, to marry him. He vowed that if he got out of this alive . . .

The creature standing over Bruno let out a deep throaty growl, then bent closer to the ground, closer to him.

Bruno made an attempt to crawl backward, but his hand caught a sharp stone on the roadway and his left arm collapsed beneath him from the pain. He had to try something else, but what?

"Please don't kill me!" he said, surprised to find that his tongue and the muscles around his mouth were working fine.

The creature stopped its advance, and for a moment its hulking body hung over Bruno like a death sentence.

"I just work for Doctor Monk, I swear," he cried. "I'm just a cameraman, for cryin' out loud!"

The creature seemed unimpressed and let out a chuff of disbelief.

Bruno felt the push of the creature's hot, sour breath against his face.

"I never wanted to take the wolf," Bruno said. "I take pictures for Monk, that's all."

The beast looked at him for a long while, as if considering what he was saying. Finally it reached down, wrapped a single hand all the way around his throat, and gave it a squeeze.

Bruno gasped, finding it hard to breathe under the pressure.

Then the beast's mouth opened and it said, "Didn't stop him."

Bruno's eyes widened in amazement. *It can talk.* The voice was monstrous, a deep rich bass that seemed to bubble up from deep within the trunk of its body. It also had trouble pronouncing the words, as if it knew all the words, but the shape of its throat and mouth made speech an arduous task.

Bruno was taking too long to answer. The creature tightened his hold on Bruno's neck, then lifted him off the ground to bring him in even closer.

"Yes, it's true I didn't, but . . ." The words came out in a string of choked and garbled syllables.

Think, think. Bruno considered telling it a lie, but something told him that might not be a good idea. The thing was big, not stupid. It wouldn't tolerate lies easily, and he didn't want to make it any more angry than it already was. Perhaps it would be best to tell the truth.

"Monk promised we'd be rich if we helped him," he said, the words still partially choked off by the iron-clad grip the beast had on his throat. "I needed the money so I went along with him."

The creature looked unconvinced.

"Monk's a powerful man. If I didn't do what he said, he could make sure I never worked again."

The creature tightened its grip on Bruno's throat once more and lifted him higher off the ground. "I can do that too," it said.

That was no doubt true. If the thing closed its hand any more tightly around Bruno's neck, his larynx and windpipe would be crushed and he'd be lucky if he ever breathed normally again, let alone worked.

"Please," Bruno said, the word coming out as a muted gurgle. "You're hurting me."

"So?"

"Please . . ." Bruno pleaded, on the verge of tears.

Just then a second creature appeared next to the first. It wasn't as big as the original, but it was just as well developed, and its fangs and claws were every bit as sharp.

The new one put a hand on the first's arm, and suddenly the grip around Bruno's neck eased.

"You can live," the second one said, its words clearer and more easily understandable than those of the first, "if you help us."

"Yeah, sure . . . anything."

"You must not tell anyone about us."

"No problem."

"If you do, we will find you."

Bruno nodded with an exaggerated gesture. "I understand."

"And you must tell people . . . Monk lies."

"Sure." That would be easy to do. "You got it."

The beast's hand was gone from Bruno's neck and he fell heavily to the ground. He let out a groan, then rolled to his left only to feel himself rising up from the ground again.

"Hey?" he said. "What's going on?"

There was no response, but Bruno realized that the bigger of the two had him by the collar of his jacket and was carrying him down the road. When they reached the tree across the roadway, Bruno was heaved over the tree, landing several yards down the road from the roadblock.

"Go," said the big one. "But remember . . . we can find you."

"Don't worry, I'll do just like you asked." Bruno got up off the road and began dusting off his clothes. "I can't stand Monk anyway."

When he finished cleaning himself off, he looked up in the direction he'd come.

The creatures were gone.

•◆•

Charles Rohan hadn't run since high school and his body was letting him know about it. When the lights had gone out, Bruno had turned back to the van while Charles had run away from it. He'd started off well enough, hurtling the tree lying across the roadway in a single bound, then sprinting off into the woods. But that had been three minutes ago and a world away. He'd gone thirty, maybe forty strides into the forest only to find himself gasping for breath. What made things worse was the uneven nature of the ground, and all of the rocks and fallen branches that were conspiring to trip him up as he ran.

His pace had slowed to little more than a jog, but the things that were chasing him didn't seem to be getting any closer. They were there, he knew, following him – stalking him. He could hear them, snapping twigs and rustling leaves as they moved. Every once in a while one of them would growl or snort, and Charles's stomach would heave and he'd have to fight the urge to vomit as he ran. They were toying with him, he realized, keeping him in their sights and waiting for him to stop running so they could tear him apart. Well, he wasn't going to let that happen. Not yet anyway.

He kept pushing forward, his lungs aching as he struggled to draw enough breath in to feed the oxygen-starved muscles of his body. His hands moved first from branch to branch and then from tree to tree as he increasingly needed their support to help keep him upright and on his feet.

A few more strides and he'd slowed to a quick walk, always reaching out for the next tree as if it were a lifeline. At last he stopped, leaning up against the trunk of a birch and sucking in lungfuls of air like a drowning man who'd just broken the surface.

Eventually the pace of his breathing slowed and he was able to hear the forest around him. It was silent. Silent except for the sound of his own breathing. He held his breath for a few seconds.

Nothing.

It was quiet. Too quiet.

Maybe I lost them? he thought, taking in a breath. He turned his head around to check, looking over his right shoulder.

"Oh my God!" he screamed.

One of them was standing no more than two feet behind him, arms crossed over its chest and – if he didn't know any better – smiling down at him.

Charles started running again, this time looking over his shoulder after every few steps just to make sure the thing wasn't following him.

When he looked again, the thing was gone. He turned back around and something solid struck him in the chest. His feet flew out from beneath him.

Clotheslined.

He landed on his back, the wind knocked out of him in a *whoosh*!

The thing – the creature – stood over him, that same smile on its face, sneering down at him like it was enjoying this stupid game of cat and mouse.

"Run!" the thing said.

It was a strange voice, as if it had to strain to get the words out. Yet the tone of it somehow sounded encouraging.

Charles didn't wait for the thing to tell him twice. He got to his feet and bolted deeper into the woods.

This time the thing followed him, walking behind him at what for it seemed to be a leisurely pace.

Charles tried to keep running, but his body was having none of it. He'd run as far as he was going to and now his legs and sides ached every bit as much as his lungs.

It can kill me if it wants to, he thought, *because I'm already dead.*

Charles toppled over, falling almost face first onto the forest floor. The ground was surprisingly soft and comfortable, and smelled of wet wood, pine needles, and autumn leaves. He closed his eyes for a moment and tried to catch his breath. That's when he felt the powerful hand grab his arm and roll him over onto his back.

"Go ahead and kill me!" he wheezed between gasps. It was going to happen anyway. Might as well get it over with now.

Nothing.

"Go ahead. Do it quick!" He squeezed his eyes shut, expecting the worst. But nothing happened.

Charles opened his eyes. The creature was kneeling by his side, looking him over from head to foot.

"Go ahead and kill me if you're going to."

The creature just looked at him.

Hope sprang into Charles's heaving chest.

"You're not going to kill me?"

The thing shrugged its shoulders, a gesture that said, "Maybe I will. Maybe I won't."

There's a chance I might live.

Charles began to breathe easier, but only slightly. But then it put a hand on his other arm and lifted him roughly off the ground.

"Hey!"

Charles was lifted higher off the ground and closer to the creature until his face was mere inches from the thing's snout. It was smelling him. *Like a cat before a meal,* he thought.

He closed his eyes, turned his head to the right and said, "Go ahead! Get it over with!"

Silence for several moments.

Charles held his breath.

He was about to open his eyes when . . . the beast roared. It was a wild and angry blast that Charles could feel all the way down in the pit of his stomach.

This is it! he thought. *The end.*

But when the roar died down and was echoing in the distant woods, Charles was still alive. In fact, the only thing he felt was exhausted. The fear had been overwhelming and now that the moment had passed, he felt drained. There was no fight left in him, not even enough to ask the thing to kill him. He just lay there, limp as a dish rag, awaiting his fate.

But instead of tearing him apart, the thing gently set him back onto the ground.

Charles opened his eyes. "What's going on?"

"You can live," the thing said in a throaty voice.

"Thank you –"

"But!" it said, almost in a bark. "This never happened."

Charles understood immediately. Monk had stumbled onto something big here, some secret that these things – werewolves he'd call them if he had to put a name to them – didn't want the rest of the world to know about. And why not? They had a right to their privacy, to their own lives. If they wanted to go public they could have done it years ago, but they decided to stay hidden in the forest, and who the hell was Monk to screw all that up for them?

For the briefest of moments, Charles considered asking the thing for money or some sort of compensation for keeping his mouth shut, but the thought was fleeting. The thing was sparing his life as it was, and if he pushed his luck, it could just as easily kill him as let him go. In the end he decided to do as it asked.

"What never happened?" he asked.

The creature's lips pulled back in another smile and it nodded. "Good."

I'm going to make it, Charles thought again. But then the creature rolled him over and picked him up by the jacket collar again. This time, it half-carried, half-dragged him through the forest back toward the road.

Instead of stopping at the road, the thing brought him to a path that cut through the woods in the direction of town. It was hard to see much of the path through the trees, but from where they were standing it looked just wide enough for a single person to walk along.

"Follow it," the thing said.

"Yeah," Charles answered, nodding his head eagerly. "Sure."

It let go of him, then gave him a gentle push along the path. Charles didn't waste any time moving and he didn't dare look back in case the thing changed its mind. He even started to run again, but this time at a much easier pace.

In minutes, Charles could see lights from the town of Redstone winking in the distance. He kept moving, knowing that he'd be all right as long as he kept on the straight and narrow path back to civilization.

Chapter 16

"Charles?"

No response.

"Bruno?"

Nothing.

Doctor Monk moved forward to peek into the cab of the van to see if either of his two men were there.

"Charles," he said in a whisper. Then, "Bruno."

They were gone.

He twisted his head around and was able to see in the direction of the driver's side. There was no one at the wheel and the door to the van was wide open.

"Where the hell could they have gone?" Monk wondered aloud. "They just had to move a tree, for cryin' out loud. How long could it take?"

But as the silence persisted, Monk began to consider the possibility that something might have happened to the two men out on the road. They were in the forest, after all. And there were all kinds of wild animals and . . . He looked back at the wolf in the cage behind him. It was staring at him, its gaze unblinking. It looked different somehow. Content. Monk studied the animal for a moment and realized that all of the fear was gone from its eyes. It was resting now, simply waiting for the situation to change – for it to be freed.

"Your friends are here, aren't they?"

The wolf didn't respond.

"What form have they taken?" Monk said. "Human? Wolf? Or perhaps . . . something in-between."

There was only the slightest reaction in the wolf's eyes, as if he'd surprised it with that last bit of speculation, but it was all he needed to let him know he was onto something.

"That is it, isn't it? You're all lycanthropes, aren't you? Werewolves! I knew it." He sat down on a chair, slapped his knee, and reveled in the moment. "Oh, this is huge. Much bigger than even I could have imagined. Just think of it, the talk shows, the television specials, books, a world-tour . . ."

The wolf in the cage growled.

"A rescue attempt!" he said. "What an excellent final chapter that will make to my book. The heroic doctor fighting off the beasts trying to stop him from bringing one of their kind to the attention of the rest of the world. What drama! What adventure!

The wolf growled again, louder this time.

"Oh, shut up!"

Monk reached for his belt and grabbed the cell phone he had clipped there. He dialed 911 and waited for an answer.

He didn't have to wait long.

"This is Doctor Edward Monk. I'm stuck inside a white cube van on Redstone Road."

"You're trapped in the vehicle and can't get out?" the female call-taker asked in a calm, detached voice.

"I can get out, it's just that . . . well, there are these were-wolves all around me."

"There are what?"

"Werewolves. They've stopped the van and now they have me trapped inside it on the road out of Redstone."

"Sir, are you aware that it is a crime to make a false 911 call?"

"This is no prank. I'm surrounded by . . ." He paused a moment to rethink his situation. "Okay then, they're wolves. I'm sorry, I was confused."

The woman said nothing for a few moments. Then, "Are you in any immediate danger?"

Monk thought about it. "No," he said, instantly regretting telling the truth.

"We can send someone to check on you."

"How long will it be?"

"I can't say, sir. Emergency services are very busy at the moment, but they'll be there as soon as they can."

"But –"

The call-taker hung up. Monk realized it could be hours before anyone came by. And all of a sudden, he wasn't as sure of himself anymore.

The wolf stared at him, as if it knew that the situation had suddenly turned and Monk was no longer the one holding the upper hand.

"What are you looking at?" he snapped.

Just then, the air was filled by the sound of something long and sharp scratching the outside of the van.

•◆•

Ranger Brock watched as the volunteer firemen from Redstone put out the last of the embers.

There was plenty of smoke, and a lot of steam as the flames were doused, but there hadn't been all that much fire.

"Well, that was easy," said Sergeant Martin as he approached Ranger Brock.

The sergeant turned and watched the firemen spread the coals with shovels to make sure the fire was completely out.

"Rather have a lot of smoke and no fire than the other way around," said Ranger Brock.

The sergeant nodded. "Me too, but . . ."

Ranger Brock waited for the sergeant to continue, but he said nothing more, leaving his words hanging in the air like the smoke from the fire.

"But what?" the ranger prodded at last.

"Oh, I don't know. It was such a neat little fire, it looked as if it might have been set on purpose."

"The thought had crossed my mind."

"Almost like a smokescreen."

Ranger Brock nodded. He'd come to the same conclusion a while ago.

"But for what?" the sergeant wondered.

The ranger had an idea about that, but he decided to keep it to himself. "Beats me," he said.

•—•

The scratching outside the van continued for several seconds. It sounded a lot like fingernails against a blackboard, but Doctor Monk knew that it wasn't fingernails doing the scratching, and instead of a blackboard the sounding board was the bare metal on the outside of the van.

Monk gritted his teeth and cringed at the sound, doing his best not to let it get under his skin. They were just trying to scare him. Well, they weren't doing that. Annoying him, yes, but scaring him? It would take a lot more than that to put fear into the heart of Doctor Edward Albert Monk. Besides, while these werewolves held the upper hand at the moment, Monk still had a few tricks up his sleeve.

Suddenly the doors at the back of the van flew open, and there were not one, not two, but *three* of the beasts, all teeth, claws, and anger.

"Don't come any closer," Monk said.

The three beasts ignored his warning and began moving into the van.

Monk pulled a handgun from the inside of his jacket and placed the overly wide barrel through one of the openings in the cage, pointing it directly at Tora, who had nowhere to run.

"I said, don't come any closer." Monk smiled, pleased that, despite his predicament, he was still able to be the one in charge. These things didn't have a clue about who they were dealing with.

"One more step and I'll shoot."

One of the beasts, the largest of the three with a pair of mismatched eyes, ignored the warning and continued forward.

"It's loaded with silver bullets I had made special for me yesterday."

That seemed to do the trick. The middle one stopped and, after a lengthy pause, backed off to join the other two. They have to be werewolves to be so afraid of silver bullets, thought Monk. Obviously the myth about silver being deadly to werewolves is true. Monk smiled. The situation seemed to be turning quite quickly in his favor.

"You see . . ." Monk paused, wondering how he should address them, and deciding on, "my lycanthropic friends. You seem to forget who you are dealing with."

The three werewolves stared at him, their gazes unblinking.

"I *know* what you are." Monk couldn't help but laugh. "I know what can kill you. And I know you have very few options in regards to myself. You can either let me go unharmed, or you must kill me. Nothing in between."

There was a slight change of expression on the middle one's face, telling Monk that he was on the right track.

"Oh sure," he continued. "You could hurt me, wound me, even leave me for dead, but unless you actually did it – you know, knocked me off, rubbed me out, tore me to shreds – there's a chance I could recover and become one of you." Again Monk laughed.

"I'd love that. Can you imagine how much I could make on the lecture circuit changing my form from wolf to man to . . . well, whatever the hell you call that shape you've got now." A pause. "Hell, forget the lecture circuit. I could do Vegas with an act like that. I'd make Céline Dion *and* Zigfried and Roy just a fond memory in that town."

The beasts did not move, but their anger over what he was saying was obvious as their lips were pulled back and their fangs glistened under the light from inside the van.

"So you freaks, you either kill me or you don't. My guess is that you haven't got it in you to kill me. If you did, I'd already be dead."

Just then the biggest of the three moved forward again. It made it halfway into the van before the middle one put an arm out to stop it.

Amazingly, the big one stopped, but not because it was overpowered. The middle-sized one seemed to have some control over it. Obviously the middle one was the leader of the three. It was a nice piece of information to know, thought Monk.

The big one eventually retreated, and in moments they were all where they'd begun, at a standoff. It stayed that way for a long while. It was obvious that something had to give, but what?

Chapter 17

Noble studied the gun in Monk's hand. It was pointed directly at Tora's head, and even if she were able to move out of the way, there was an excellent chance that some part of the bullet might catch her. And as they all knew, any piece of silver entering any part of a werewolf's body would be fatal. Even a flesh wound would be disastrous, and Noble wasn't about to risk Tora's life just to get his talons on the likes of Doctor Monk.

Noble glanced to his right and noticed Argus looking at him, the expression on his face asking the very same question. Argus no doubt wanted to rush forward, tear Monk apart, and break Tora out of the cage, but it was only love for his sister that was holding him back. None of them would risk Tora that way. She'd already suffered enough at the hands of this man.

Noble turned to his left and saw that Harlan was trying to get his attention. At first Noble wasn't sure what his smaller brother was trying to tell him, but he noticed that Harlan was holding his right hand close to his chest, three fingers curled into the palm, the index finger extended and the thumb standing straight up. He had formed his hand into the shape of a gun.

What's up with that? Noble wondered. His gaze moved from Harlan's hand to his face.

Harlan was shaking his head.

Noble still didn't understand.

Then Harlan gestured toward Monk.

Noble looked in that direction and for the first time paid particular attention to Monk's gun. It didn't look like a regular gun. It was *shaped* like a regular handgun with a grip, trigger, and barrel, but the proportions were all wrong. It seemed big and lumpy in Monk's hand, and the barrel was two, maybe three times bigger than what you would expect on a handgun. Suddenly Noble realized it wasn't a real gun at all. In fact, the longer Noble studied it, the more obvious it became that the weapon was nothing more than a flare gun, very similar in design and appearance as the one Ranger Brock carried in the back of his 4 x 4.

"You're not going to stand there all day, are you?" Monk asked.

The hair down Noble's back bristled in anger.

"Because I really should be on my way."

Noble could feel his brothers were just as anxious to do something as he was.

"If you don't mind, close the doors on your way out."

Harlan let out a low growl.

"And clear the road while you're out there. I'm late enough as it is already."

That was it. Noble couldn't stand it anymore. He'd had enough of Doctor Monk, and the time had come to end this once and for all.

Noble leapt forward.

Argus and Harlan followed.

Monk pulled the gun away from the cage. . . .

And fired.

Chapter 18

Harlan was right. Monk's weapon was a flare gun. The flare came out of the muzzle in a flash of brilliant red heat.

All three of them retreated, but the flare caught Noble in the shoulder, knocking him backward out of the van. Noble hit the ground with a thud, the flare landing on the ground next to him, the flame of the flare pointed in his direction, searing his flesh and burning away most of the fur across his shoulder, neck, and the outside of his right arm. He rolled to the right, away from the flare, smoke rising up from his burnt shoulder.

Even though he was away from the flare, the pain left by its flame was excruciating, as if his shoulder were being sliced open by a thousand red-hot knives. Noble let out a wail that was halfway between a scream and a cry for help.

The flare continued to burn, casting an eerie red light on the scene and filling the air with thick gray smoke. Through the reddish haze, Noble saw Monk leap from the van.

Argus turned to chase after him, but Noble told him, "Never mind him. Get Tora!"

A moment later, Argus was pulling the cage from the van with Tora still inside it.

Harlan appeared by Noble's side, grabbing the flare before it set the grass and brush by the side of the road on fire. The flare continued to smoke and sizzled with a blinding red light. Harlan held it out in front of him like a torch for several seconds then, without anywhere else to put it, tossed it back into the empty van. He closed the doors to the vehicle, locking them shut.

Noble closed his eyes and did his best not to think about the pain in his shoulder. It seemed an impossible task, especially since the air was full of the pungent smell of sulfur and his own burnt flesh. Somehow Noble was able to smile through the pain.

To his right he could hear Argus using his bare hands to tear apart the cage that had held Tora for the last couple of days. And then the happy sounds of a reunion between sister and brothers.

They'd done it. Noble breathed easier. Already the pain in his shoulder seemed to be fading.

But then Harlan said, "We must get away!"

Noble opened his eyes and saw that the flare had ignited something inside the van. Smoke was now leaking out of the vehicle through the seams around the door. Within minutes the entire van would be engulfed in flames.

"You want me to carry you?" Argus asked, kneeling at Noble's side.

"No," he answered. "I can make it." Noble tried to get up, but his shoulder wouldn't co-operate. "But I could use a hand," he added.

Argus grabbed Noble's left arm and pulled.

Noble was on his feet. His knees felt weak and rubbery, but he could walk.

Harlan was already leading Tora away.

Noble and Argus followed them –

Into the forest.

•—•

Doctor Monk stopped running for a moment to pull his cell phone from inside his jacket. For the second time in half an hour, he dialed 911. When a call-taker answered, he said, "This is Doctor Edward Monk again. I called before, remember."

"Your call is in the queue, Mr. Monk. Someone should be there soon."

"Well, now it's on fire!"

"What's on fire, sir?"

"My van. I shot one of the wolves with a flare and another one threw it back into the van."

"A wolf threw the flare you shot at it back into your vehicle?"

"Yes!"

A pause. "Are you out of the vehicle now, sir?"

"Of course I'm out of the vehicle."

"Is the vehicle still on Redstone Road."

"What's left of it."

"Emergency services have been dispatched."

"When will they get here?"

"Your call has been upgraded to a priority one, sir. They should be there shortly."

Monk disconnected and put the phone back in his pocket.

"Sure, now that there's some danger of the forest going up in flames, they're right on it." He looked around for something to sit on and made himself comfortable on a fallen log. "I guess I'll just wait for them to show up and get a ride into town."

But as he watched the van burn for a moment, he noticed that its fire was casting light into the forest. He looked down at his arms and legs and realized his clothes were brightly illuminated by the fire and he'd be easy to spot among the trees. If someone, or some*thing* were looking for him, he'd be pretty easy to find.

"Or maybe not," he said, getting up from the log and running. Away from the fire – and into the forest.

Chapter 19

When they were far enough away from the burning van, the four werewolves found a clearing in the forest where they could rest.

Tora was the first to find comfort on the cool, moist humus of the forest floor. In human form now, she sat down and stretched her legs, her three brothers – still werewolves, but a little closer to human form to allow them easier speech – gathered around her like a captive audience.

"How are you?" asked Noble.

"I'm tired," she said, her smile stretching from ear to ear. "Very, very tired." Then she must have noticed Noble's shoulder, because her eyes went wide a moment and she said, "How are *you*?"

Noble rotated his right arm and cringed at the pain that went shooting up through his shoulder and down the length of his arm. "Just a flesh wound," he said, doing his best not to let them know how much he was hurting. "Besides, it'll heal quick enough."

That much was true. One benefit of being able to change their shape was that any tissue that had been damaged in one shape would be reorganized and repaired during the shape shifting process. A single change into human form and the wound would almost be healed over. A few more changes and he'd be as good as new, but with a scar to remind him of the ordeal.

"I was beginning to wonder if you were ever going to come for me."

"We gave the humans every chance to save you," Harlan said. "When they failed, then it was our turn." Argus gave his little brother a stiff, yet friendly punch in the arm, then said, "Noble made us wait for the right moment, that's all."

"Yeah," Harlan agreed, rubbing his sore arm. "We had to make sure the time was right, you know . . . so everything would turn out okay."

"And," Noble said, "we had to make sure we had the help of Michael Martin."

"Michael," she said, her smile seeming to grow even wider, a hint of a sparkle entering her tired eyes. "He helped you?"

Noble nodded. "Couldn't have done it without him."

"He was key," Argus added.

"And he did a great job, too."

Tora took a deep breath and let out a long contented sigh.

Noble looked at his two brothers and each one of them was smiling, sharing a small part of their sister's moment of happiness.

"When can I see him?"

"Hold on," said Noble. "We've got to get you home first. Phyllis is worried sick about you, and Ranger Brock will want to know you're all right."

Tora nodded. "I could use some sleep."

They all got up from the ground and started out for home. After just a few steps, Tora said, "What happened to Doctor Monk?"

"He got away!" Argus said, his displeasure over that particular turn of events evident in his voice.

"We wanted you back safe. That's all that mattered," Noble explained.

Tora stopped in her tracks.

The others took a few more steps, then stopped as well.

"He's got tapes," she said.

"What?"

"Tapes. Video tapes. He has images of me changing my shape, and another one of all of us changing form in the forest."

Noble lowered his head and turned it slightly to the side, deep in thought.

"We can't let him get those tapes back to the city," Harlan said.

"He was talking about a television special, maybe a feature film . . . all based on what was on the tapes."

"Never mind television," Harlan said. "He could have the images up on the Internet tonight. Within a day or two, people all over the world would know about us."

Argus's hands suddenly balled into fists. "We can't let him do that."

Noble shook his head. "Of course not."

"Then what are we going to do about it?"

⚫

Sergeant Martin pulled up beside Ranger Brock and rolled down his window.

"We've got another call from Doctor Monk," the sergeant said.

"Still trapped inside his van?"

The sergeant shook his head. "No. It's on fire now."

Ranger Brock felt his heart leap up into his throat. "Is the wolf still inside it?"

"All we know is that Monk's not inside it."

The ranger didn't say another word. Instead he got into his vehicle and followed the sergeant to the fire. Although the sergeant was driving as fast as he could with all of his lights and sirens wailing, it wasn't fast enough for Ranger Brock. Years ago, he'd seen a very special wolf die in a forest fire. He didn't want to see one of its offspring die the same way.

⚫

"We *have* to go after him," Noble said. "We can't let him have those tapes."

"Then let's go!" said Tora.

Noble put a hand on her. "Hold on! You're not going anywhere."

As Noble expected, Tora didn't argue. He knew that she wanted nothing more than to go after the doctor and exact her revenge, but her body wasn't up to the task. After her ordeal, she'd need a couple of days' rest before being ready to take on the world again.

He looked at Harlan. "And one of us will have to take you home, to make sure you get there safely."

"Why are you looking at me when you say that?" Harlan wanted to know.

"I thought you might want to take your sister home."

"Why me, though?"

"It's an important job."

"Why don't you take her?" he said. "You're hurt. You need to go home yourself."

Noble didn't respond to that even though Harlan had an excellent point. Noble had been injured and his ability to move, maybe even to think, had been affected. But while Noble wasn't a hundred per cent, if he took Tora home then that would leave Harlan and Argus to handle Monk on their own and he was sure neither of the two wanted to do that.

"And I'm your best tracker. How are you going to find Monk out there without me?"

Another good point. But the truth was that Monk's scent wouldn't be all that hard to follow. It was fresh and more than likely strong, full of sweat, sloughed skin cells, and just a touch of fear.

"You're right, Harlan," Noble said. "You are the best tracker, but Monk hasn't gone that far. Any one of us could find him easily enough."

"But I want to go after Monk!" Harlan continued, a lot of his initial indignation seeming to fade with the realization that Noble, as always, knew what he was doing. "I want a piece of him, just like you do."

"I know you do," said Noble.

Finally, perhaps sensing Noble needed help in this situation, Argus stepped forward and said, "I'd be happy to take Tora home."

Harlan's face was a mask of surprise. "You would?"

Argus looked at Tora and smiled. "Of course I would. In fact, I'd be honored. Just the thought of seeing Phyllis's face when I walk through the door with Tora would be worth it."

Noble glanced over at Harlan, hoping Argus's ploy would have the desired effect.

"No, that's okay, I'll do it."

"Okay," Argus said, his voice dripping with sincerity. "But only if you really want to."

"You can stop acting now, big man," Harlan smirked. "I've already agreed to do it."

Argus laughed.

"All right, now that that's settled," Noble interjected. "Let's move."

Harlan took Tora's arm and began escorting her home.

Noble and Argus headed in the opposite direction, in search of a mad doctor named Monk.

Chapter 20

"They can't hurt me," Doctor Monk whispered under his breath, between gasps for air. "If they hurt me, I'll become one of them."

He'd exited the forest and was now running along the road, at a pace no faster than a brisk walk. His head was continuously swiveling around on his shoulders on the lookout for one of the creatures, but he couldn't see a one.

"They can't hurt me," he said again, believing it more and more each time he said it.

They were werewolves, these creatures, and if they hurt him, if they wounded him and opened up his flesh and he survived, then according to what little he knew of werewolf lore, he would become a werewolf himself.

Edo van Belkom

How bad would that be? he wondered. If he were a were-wolf, he wouldn't need anything from them. Not a wolf, and certainly not any videotape. If he were a werewolf himself, then he could change his shape whenever he wanted. Imagine, he thought, an entire television special based on a dramatic live transformation from human to wolf form, then back again. Some pretty popular shows had been built up around a lot less. And then, after the television show aired, he could move to Las Vegas where he could do four shows a night, five on Sundays. Then there were private shows for corporations and Arab sheiks. The possibilities were endless.

If only they hurt him, and if they let him survive. Those were two pretty big *ifs*. They were going to hurt him, that was for sure. But would they let him live? He very much doubted that these creatures would want him to become one of them, especially after what he had tried to do with one of their kind. So they were likely going to kill him. The thought sent a spike of fear shooting down Monk's spine.

Of course they were going to kill him. What else could they do to him that would be a just punishment for trying to snatch one of them away from its family? Kidnapping. If he'd tried to do the same thing to a human that's what they'd call it. But these things, these werewolves, were more than human, and their brand of justice was probably more than human justice would allow.

Monk kept up his pace, his legs aching from the run and his lungs feeling as if they were at the bursting point.

"Serves you right," he wheezed. "Biggest discovery of your career and you're thinking about television specials and Las Vegas shows . . ." He slowed to a walk to catch his breath. "What if Doctor David Suzuki had found these things? He'd be interested in their genetic code, their DNA. Research, research, research! But you, Doctor Edward Monk, the first thing that comes to your mind is a circus sideshow. No wonder no one ever takes you seriously."

Just then Monk heard a sound off to his right – a low throaty growl, like from an angry dog. Only this thing sounded much bigger than a dog, and much angrier.

"Who's there?" Monk said to the darkness.

•—•

Harlan had "borrowed" a blanket and a sheet from a clothesline in the backyard of a house they'd passed along the way. He and Tora could have returned home as wolves then changed into human form just before entering the house, but Harlan hadn't wanted Tora to arrive completely naked following her ordeal. Somehow it just didn't seem right.

When they reached the house, Harlan opened the door for Tora and followed her inside.

"Hello?" he said.

"Harlan?" answered Phyllis. "Is that you?"

"I've got Tora," he said.

"What?" The word was accompanied by the sound of rushing feet.

"I said, I've got –"

Phyllis was there in the hallway. Her eyes, locked on Tora, suddenly went wide and maybe just a little bit wet.

"Hi!" Tora said.

"Are you all right?"

Tora nodded.

"Let's get you cleaned up," Phyllis said, taking Tora by the hand and leading her down the hall. "How does a nice hot bath sound?"

"That sounds good."

"Or do you want something to eat first?"

Tora answered, but their voices were too faint now for Harlan to understand. He took a deep breath and sighed with satisfaction. Tora was in good hands now. She'd be well taken care of and back to normal in no time.

Harlan turned for the door. Maybe he could return the blanket and sheet before anyone realized they were missing. Then he'd track down Noble and Argus.

If he were lucky, he might get to them before they were finished with the good Doctor Monk.

•◆•

"Who's there?" Monk said again.

At first there was no answer, then another growl cut through the silence, its source much closer than before.

Monk felt his heart leap up into his throat. He tried to swallow, but his mouth was too dry to do anything but pant.

Suddenly, movement to his left. The swish of a tree branch. The crack of a dead twig underfoot.

"You can't hurt me!" Monk said, as loud as he could.

"You know what will happen if you hurt me, don't you?" A pause. "I wouldn't mind, but I don't think you'd want that. Right?"

He paused again, waiting for an answer. When none came, he continued.

"So your only choice is to *kill* me."

Hearing himself saying the words almost made Monk throw up. His stomach heaved, but he constricted his throat as best he could, fighting off his body's urge to vomit. Moments later the feeling had passed and he was able to continue.

"You're not killers, are you?" he said, gaining confidence with every word. "If you were I would have been dead a long time ago."

Another pause.

In the silence he could hear things moving in the woods all around him. He was sure it was the creatures. Two of them, maybe more. They were circling him, and maybe, just maybe, his talk was having some effect because it seemed to Monk that they were stalling in order to buy some time to figure out what they wanted to do with him.

"And I didn't kill the wolf, did I? So killing me just wouldn't be right. The only alternative you have is to let me go. I promise I won't tell anybody anything about what I've seen in these woods." Monk shrugged. "I'll be on my way and it'll be as if none of this ever happened. What do you say?"

One more pause, this one the longest yet.

"Well?"

The woods suddenly erupted with a swishing sound, as if something large was slicing through the forest, brushing past every tree and leaf along the way.

Monk turned to try and see where the noise was coming from. When he finally saw it, it was too late to do anything but wait for the moment of impact.

It was a stout tree branch, roughly ten feet long and nearly a foot around. The creature wielded it like some giant baseball bat, the end of it skimming over the earth and mowing down small brush and saplings in its path.

Monk's only thought was *How strong can these things be?* And then the branch connected with his legs, taking them out from under him and knocking him hard onto the ground, as if he were nothing more than a blade of grass caught in the path of a scythe.

All at once, the realization hit Monk like a hammer blow to the base of his brain. *They can hurt me without even touching me.*

"Please, no!" he screamed. "I'll do whatever you want, just don't hurt me."

"The tapes," one of the things said in a throaty voice.

For a moment, Monk was awestruck by the fact that these creatures were capable of speech.

"I said, the tapes."

"What tapes?" Monk said, struggling to get the words out.

The smaller of the two glanced over at the larger one wielding the tree branch and nodded. Without hesitation, the bigger one raised the branch and brought it crashing down onto Monk's legs.

Pain flared in Monk's thighs, but nothing seemed to be broken. Obviously they were being very careful about what they did to him. They probably wouldn't mortally wound him, but they wouldn't spare him any agony until they got what they wanted.

Monk wasn't sure if he was up to the challenge, but he wasn't about to give up anything without a fight.

"I don't have any tapes," he said, his voice crackling with fear despite his best efforts to stay calm.

"You lie!"

"I'm not lying, I swear."

The tree branch came at him again, this time hitting him hard in the stomach. The wind rushed from his body in a *whoosh* and he was left doubled over and gasping for breath like a fish out of water. Then, before he was able to catch his breath, there were hands on him. Strong hands, turning him back around, opening his coat, searching him for –

"Ah!" one of them grunted.

"Liar!" said the other, holding one of the tapes in the air like a prize.

Monk shook his head. "I didn't know that was in there. I swear."

They searched through his jacket and found the other tapes. The smaller of the two creatures brought the three tapes in close to Monk's face, then stared at him as if waiting for an explanation.

"Those were in my coat?" Monk asked, his voice innocent and as dumbfounded as he could make it.

The bigger one grabbed Monk by the hair and lifted his head off the ground so he could get a closer look at the tapes.

"Well, it's possible I was carrying an extra tape or two for Bruno. See, he's not a very good cameraman and uses up far more tape than he –"

The creature forced Monk's head back to the ground in disgust, then searched the rest of him for more tapes. There were none.

Monk watched the tapes, his only proof of these creatures' existence he had, tucked smartly up under the left arm of the smaller of the two werewolves.

Gone!

The tapes were gone now and there was nothing more they could do to hurt him. His career, his life, was over. He'd gone into the woods to shoot a segment on forest regeneration after a fire and he'd succeeded only in getting his equipment destroyed and losing his crew in the forest. He didn't even have the regeneration segment to sell to the Discovery Channel. Good luck trying to sell them anything else anytime soon. Meanwhile, Suzuki has probably lined up a half-dozen specials and a revival of that stupid show he does for the CBC.

"Go ahead!" Monk screamed. "Do it!"

The two werewolves pulled back slightly, then looked at each other a moment.

"Go on and kill me!" He was on the verge of tears. "Just get it over with!"

Seconds passed without movement or sound.

Monk prepared himself for death. The end of his life.

He took a deep breath and held it. Waited . . . but nothing happened. Except for something warm and wet running down the inside of his leg.

Great! thought Monk, realizing he'd wet himself. *What a perfect ending to this whole ordeal.*

Suddenly, there were hands on the collar of Monk's jacket and he was lifted until only his shoes touched the ground. Then he was moving, his feet dragging along the ground as the two creatures pulled him along as easily as a human might drag a piece of string over a hardwood floor.

"Hey, hey," Monk said. "What's going on?"

But there was no answer. They continued dragging him through the woods, bumping him roughly over rocks and fallen logs. His left shoe came off first, but the right one hung on for at least ten more minutes.

His legs eventually began to ache, and the bottoms of his feet were rubbed raw, but the werewolves didn't seem to care about his condition one way or the other. In fact, they didn't slow their pace one bit until they stopped dead in their tracks and unceremoniously dropped him onto his back.

"Hey!" he said, rolling over onto his stomach.

Without a word, they grabbed him by the arms and lifted him onto his feet. Monk wobbled a moment, then managed to stand on his own. The town of Redstone stretched out before him, less than a quarter mile away.

"What do you want me to do now?" Monk said.

There was no answer. He turned left and right, looking for the two creatures, but they were gone. Monk took a deep breath – and began limping toward town.

Chapter 21

"Who's out there?" The voice came from the back door of the house.

Harlan didn't dare answer because he knew who the voice belonged to. He hadn't thought much about it before, but he now realized the blanket and sheet he'd borrowed belonged to an old-timer named Dallas Ketchum. Dallas had lived in these woods for more than fifty years and had made his living by trapping and logging and just about everything in between.

"You stealin' clothes off my line?" he said.

Harlan said nothing, concentrating only on the clothespins in his hands. He was trying to hang up the sheet and blanket in the same place he'd found them, but now that the old man knew he was there, Harlan would be happy just getting them back on the line.

"You wait right there while I get my gun!"

Harlan placed the last of the clothespins on the line and ran as fast as he could toward the forest. When he reached the safety of the trees, he turned and saw Dallas standing at his back door with a shotgun in one hand and a flashlight in the other.

In the dim light cast by the man's flashlight, Harlan could also see the sheet and blanket he'd hung up on the line. They were both hanging crooked with one end attached to the line and the other dragging back and forth across the ground.

"You crazy kids!" he said.

"Sorry," Harlan muttered under his breath. He hated to inconvenience the old man, but if he hadn't been so quick to defend his property, his laundry would have been returned to the line with no one the wiser.

Harlan made a mental note to do something nice for the old-timer as soon as he had the chance.

"Harlan!"

There was someone behind him. He hoped it wasn't Dallas Ketchum.

"Harlan, it's us."

Harlan let out a sigh of relief, then turned to see Noble and Argus standing there in their werewolf form. Noble had the video tapes under his arm and, judging by the grins on their faces, everything went well with Doctor Monk.

"How did it go with the doctor?" Harlan asked.

Noble took the tapes from under his arm and showed them to Harlan. "We got the tapes," he said.

"And Monk peed his pants."

Harlan laughed. "Excellent!"

•◆•

When they got home, Noble, Argus, and Harlan all wanted to check in on Tora, but Phyllis was having none of it.

"She's resting now. Out like a log," she said, ushering them past Tora's room as if she were herding sheep. "I know she'd want to see you, but you'd only get her excited again."

"But we just want to –" Harlan said.

"No *buts*." she said with a wave of her hand. From her tone, it was obvious that there would be no room for compromise on this one. "Busy yourselves for an hour or two, then you can see her . . . maybe."

Reluctantly, they agreed. But Noble, like the others, was a bit too wound up just to sit around the house and watch television or play video games. And Ranger Brock wouldn't be home for hours himself, no doubt having all sorts of paperwork and explaining to do after what happened to Doctor Monk and his men. So instead of hanging around, the boys decided to head to one of their favorite spots – a partial clearing a hundred yards up one of the mountains of the Nechako range where they could gaze up at the moon and lord over the forest that stretched out like a deep green shag carpet at their feet.

When they arrived, Argus gathered together several handfuls of dry sticks and pine needles, and Harlan moved several stones into a rough circle on top of a rocky patch in the clearing. When the fire pit was ready, Harlan struck a match and ignited the needles at the base of the pit. Within minutes a roaring fire was burning, perfect for their needs.

Noble waited until there was a good bed of coals fueling the fire, then brought out the videotapes he'd taken from Doctor Monk. Then, one by one, he dropped them into the pit.

It took a while for the first one to catch fire, but when it did, green-blue flames leapt up from the pit like flickering neon. The burning plastic was giving off an acrid black smoke that, luckily, no one could see in the dark of night.

Twenty minutes later, all of the videotapes had been reduced to blobs of bubbling black goo. Noble picked up a stick and prodded the blobs to make sure each of the tapes – and the images they contained – had been destroyed. They had.

Argus threw a new log on the fire and they settled in to watch the yellow orange flames leap and dance.

"I'm glad everything turned out okay," said Harlan, lying on his back and trying to make his head comfortable against a pillow-sized rock.

"We were lucky," Noble said, then corrected himself. "*Tora* was lucky everything worked out in the end."

"You know who's really lucky?" said Argus.

"Who?" Harlan was sitting up now, turning over the rock in an attempt to find a smoother, perhaps even softer, side, without any luck.

"That creep Monk." Argus nearly spat the name as he said it. "If you ask me, he got off way too easy."

"Maybe," was all Noble said. He didn't think Monk had gotten off easy at all, but he wasn't about to contradict Argus and detract from the moment. They had saved their sister. Even better, they had rescued her from imprisonment at the hand of three malicious humans. And on top of all that, they had left the evil Doctor Monk a psychological wreck. The doctor would require weeks to recover, and things would likely be quiet in the forest for the next little while. Sure, Argus had wanted to physically hurt the doctor, maybe even kill him, but Noble had an idea that letting the doctor go unharmed was probably the worst punishment of all.

"I don't mean we should have killed him," Argus went on. "And I know if we had hurt him and passed along the taint, we risked making him a lycanthrope like us . . . and that would have been bad."

"Very bad," Harlan commented.

Noble nodded. "Yes."

"But I would have liked to do something to him, like . . . like . . ." Argus gazed up at the moon as if the punishment he sought was written across the stars in some sort of code. "Like cut his tongue out so he could never tell anyone about us and what we are."

Noble's grin was ear to ear.

Argus must have looked at Noble and noticed his smile, because he poked him in the arm and said, "What's so funny?"

"It's an interesting idea, but I think the doctor should tell everyone about us, as many people as he can."

"What?"

Noble nodded. "I'm counting on it, in fact."

Argus scratched his head in doubt, but Harlan giggled with understanding.

Doctor Monk looked ragged and bruised, as if he needed the help of a doctor. There was a welt over his right eye, a yellowish-purple bruise on his left cheek, and he was holding his left leg as if it were broken. What's more, what little hair he had on his head seemed to have turned a bit whiter in the past few hours.

Seeing the doctor like this, with a wild, wide-eyed look of fear in his eyes, made Sergeant Martin think, *What the hell happened out there in the forest?*

With the doctor's condition in mind, the sergeant had asked Monk if he'd like to visit the hospital first. But the man was adamant that he wanted to file a complaint with the RCMP before he did anything else.

Now they were in the detachment's modest interview room, sitting across from each other at a round gray table and having a little chat. Monk had originally wanted to start talking in the cruiser, but the sergeant had told him not to say a word until they reached the detachment. The interview room had a video camera attached to three

VCRs, each one making a copy of the interview. It was better this way, the sergeant thought, because from what the doctor had been hinting at, it might be best that he got it all on tape rather than making notes in his book.

"Comfortable?" asked the sergeant.

Monk shifted in his chair, wincing in pain with each tiny movement of his body. "No," he answered.

Sergeant Martin ignored him.

"Right, then. Why don't you tell me what happened."

"We were on our way to the main highway, driving nice and slow . . . you know, to be careful."

The sergeant nodded.

"Then we stopped because a big tree had fallen down across the road."

"That happens a lot in the forest."

"But it didn't just fall down. It was cut, or broken, or I don't know what. But it was there across the road *on purpose*."

"It would be kind of hard to prove something like that. I mean, that it had been put there on purpose."

Monk shook his head in frustration. "They put it there because they didn't want me leaving with the wolf."

The sergeant sat up. "Who's *they*?"

Monk sighed. "Oh, c'mon. You know who they are. You and that ranger know exactly what I'm talking about."

Sergeant Martin opened his eyes a bit wider and shook his head slightly. "Haven't a clue, Doctor Monk. Who are they? And what are you talking about?"

Monk sighed again, only this time the frustration was beginning to show on his face. "The werewolves," he said. "The forest here is full of them, and the wolf I had was one of them."

"Really," the sergeant said, narrowing his eyes and looking more closely at the doctor's head for any signs of trauma.

"Yes, really. Do you think I would go through all of this trouble just for a stupid wolf?"

The sergeant nodded. "But you didn't mention anything about werewolves before. You just said it was some sort of special wolf."

"Of course that's what I said," Monk said. "Who would have let me take a werewolf out of the forest?"

"So you were lying before?"

"No."

"Then you're lying now."

"No."

"But you've changed your story, so one of them's got to be a lie, right?"

"Yes . . . No! All right, maybe I bent the truth before a bit. That wolf was special. It was a werewolf. Follow me?"

The sergeant nodded again, feigning understanding. Then he pointed to his right and said. "I want you to look in that direction and start again from the beginning, and leave nothing out. Nothing."

The doctor began telling his story again.

Sergeant Martin glanced over his shoulder into the

other room just to make sure the doctor was looking directly into the camera. This was a tape for the ages, and the rest of the officers in the detachment were going to be rolling on the floor after watching this one.

•-•·

The boys returned home shortly after ten, ready for some sleep. As they entered the house, Phyllis was in the kitchen preparing a tray for Tora, with a steaming mug of hot chocolate and a plate of oversized chocolate chip cookies.

Argus reached for one of the cookies, only to have his hand slapped away by Phyllis.

"There's more in the cupboard," she said.

Argus rubbed his hand as if it hurt.

"And the milk's still warm so if you'd like some hot chocolate, you're welcome to make it."

Harlan looked as if he were about to say something about Tora getting room service, but Noble cut him off.

"Is she awake?" he asked. "Can we see her now?"

Phyllis smiled. "She's awake and back to normal, as far as I can tell."

"She's tough," said Argus, with a tone that suggested he was proud of his sister.

They followed Phyllis into the room. Tora's face brightened with a broad smile the moment she saw them enter the room.

As Phyllis put down the tray, the boys gathered round their sister giving her hugs and kisses and doing their best not to shed any tears.

Tora's eyes were wet and glassy. "Thanks, guys," she said.

"No problem," Harlan mumbled.

"Hey," Argus said with a wave.

Noble couldn't help but laugh at how awkward his brothers were finding the situation. "It was nothing you wouldn't have done for us," he said.

Harlan and Argus nodded vigorously as if to say, "What he said."

"But I still don't fully understand what took so long," she said, taking a mug of hot chocolate from Phyllis in one hand and a cookie in the right."

"We had to wait," said Argus, the disgust still evident in his voice.

"We had to wait until Ranger Brock and the others had tried all of the proper channels," Noble said, not waiting for Argus to explain the situation fully. "They tried everything they could, but Doctor Monk just had too many friends in high places."

"But you're here now," Harlan piped up. "And that's all that matters."

"Yes," Noble sighed.

"That's right," added Argus, putting one of his big hands gently on Tora's shoulder.

Tora sipped her hot chocolate, then said, "I'll even be back to school on Monday."

Harlan laughed. "Oh, won't Michael Martin be glad to see you."

"Have you heard from him?" Tora asked, her eyes going wide with excitement.

"No, not yet," Harlan said.

"But we'll call him tonight," Noble said quickly. "You know, just to let him know you're all right."

Tora smiled. "You think he would want to know if I was okay or not?"

The brothers all looked at each other, allowing themselves only the barest hint of a smile.

"Okay," Phyllis broke in. "That's enough for now. You boys get to bed before you get the girl all starry-eyed."

Harlan began to giggle, but a sharp jab in the ribs from Argus cut the laughter off in his throat.

They said good night to Tora and left her room for their own.

Once in their own bedroom, Noble said, "Mention of school reminded me of something."

Harlan sat up on his bed, "What's up?"

Noble came over and sat on the side of Harlan's bed. "Can you get into the school's computer?"

"No problem."

"And change the attendance record to show that Tora was present the past two days."

Harlan got up off his bed and switched on his computer. "That's easy," he said.

"Better yet, just mark her present for the rest of the week."

"But the week's not over yet," said Argus.

Harlan looked over his shoulder at them and smiled devilishly. "You think that makes a difference to me?"

"You can do that?" Argus asked, obviously impressed.

"Oh, I can do a lot of things to the school computer."

"Grades, for one, class schedules, teacher assignments, student suspensions . . ."

"You can change grades?" Argus was still stuck on this one point.

"Just Tora's attendance," Noble said, coming up behind Argus and looking over Harlan's shoulder at the computer screen."

"But I could sure do with a better mark in math class," Argus said.

Noble shook his head.

Argus clenched his hands into fists and rested them on his hips. "Let me get this straight. It's okay to use the computer to help Tora, but not me."

Noble shook his head. "It's not really okay for either one. In fact, it's sort of like our ability to change our shape."

"What do you mean?" asked Argus.

"It's a special thing, and it's better to save it for those times when we really need it."

Argus looked confused.

"Like making sure we all graduate," Harlan said.

"Exactly," said Noble.

"What?" Argus looked around. "You really think I'm going to graduate."

Harlan smiled as his fingers flashed and clicked over the keyboard. "I don't think," he said. "I know."

Noble slapped his big brother on the shoulder. "We don't leave anybody behind," he said. "Not in the forest, and not in the eleventh grade."

All Argus could do was grin.

"Done," Harlan said.

"Okay," said Noble. "Now get offline so I can call Michael Martin and tell him his sweetheart's doing fine."

Harlan and Argus laughed . . . but only a little.

Chapter 22

Two days later, Redstone played host to a camera team from the television tabloid program *Inside Entertainment Weekly*. The crew had come to Redstone all the way from Toronto looking for evidence to support Doctor Monk's claims that the woods surrounding Redstone were full of werewolves. If they were successful, the piece would be expanded from a ten-minute news feature to an hour-long special.

The show's star reporter, Arlessa Delfin, was a blue-eyed blond from the city. In a tight business suit and high heels, she looked absolutely out of place in the interior of British Columbia. What's more, she asked questions as if the fate of the nation were riding on every answer. Obviously, she took her job seriously, even though many of the people she interviewed didn't share her opinion about the importance of the subject matter she was covering for her show.

When she interviewed Sergeant Martin, the question she kept coming back to was this: "Are there werewolves living in the forests around Redstone, as Doctor Monk claims?"

In response to the question, Sergeant Martin smiled, laughed slightly under his breath, and said, "I've been patrolling these woods for almost twenty years and I've seen all kinds of things from killer rabbits to rabid bears, from abandoned babies to mountain men, but I've never, ever in my life seen a werewolf or even heard talk of one stalking these woods."

"But Doctor Monk is a man of science. If he were making all of this up – and I'm not saying he is – then why would he choose Redstone when he could have chosen any part of the country he pleased?"

The sergeant shrugged. "I haven't got a clue. He might have latched on to a bit of local folklore and decided to run with it, but that's a question Doctor Monk should be answering for himself."

·-·-·

Arlessa Delfin and her crew had spent an entire morning setting up a makeshift studio in the parking lot of the Redstone Inn. At two in the afternoon, she would be sitting in one of the chairs set up in the middle of the lot while Doctor Edward Monk would be sitting across from her in another. At that time of the day the sun would be shining magnificently on the summits of the mountains to the west and would give her interview the sort of larger-than-life backdrop that the man's claims demanded.

Werewolves in British Columbia.

The more doctor Monk insisted werewolves existed, the less evidence she was able to find to support his assertion. When she contacted the two men who had last worked for Monk, both of them had said he was as loony as a Canadian dollar and couldn't be persuaded to say anything else even when the show's producers offered them cash if they'd back up Monk's statements. Both of the men turned down the show's request for an on-camera interview, even hanging up before they could double the amount of money they were offering.

So here they were, interviewing the good doctor without a single shred of evidence to back up his claim of there being lycanthropes in the forest. If they were lucky, maybe they could salvage what they had and portray the doctor as a sad sort of madman who believes what he says to be true no matter what others say to the contrary.

After all, there have been people who have made careers out of claiming Elvis Presley is still alive, that they've been abducted by aliens, or have been someone else in a previous life. None of those people ever had the slightest bit of proof to back up their stories – and no one seemed to care one way or the other. Even that famous film footage of Bigfoot walking through the forest in Washington State had been proven to be a fake years ago, but there were still people who refused to believe the whole thing had been a hoax. Why should this be any different?

Doctor Edward Monk said there were werewolves in the forest in these parts. He couldn't prove there were. No one could prove there weren't. A lot of pretty successful shows had had less to go on.

And so, when the sun was in the right spot and the light on the mountains behind them was just right, Arlessa Delfin began interviewing Doctor Edward Monk about his theories.

He recounted the story of what happened to him in these woods, how he and his crew accidentally videotaped the werewolves changing form in the middle of a clearing.

"Where's that tape now?" Ms. Delfin asked, her face lighting up with anticipation.

"The werewolves took it from me," he said.

"I see."

Doctor Monk continued talking, explaining to the young reporter how he and his men had captured the wolf and recorded images of it changing shape while in their custody.

"Where's the wolf now, Doctor Monk?"

"It was rescued by the other three werewolves."

A pause. "I see, and the tape?"

"They took it from me along with the other one."

Another pause, this one longer than the first. Although Arlessa Delfin prided herself on being a true professional, it was hard to take this man seriously when his face was still swollen and bruised and there were bandages over both his right eye and his nose.

"Doctor Monk, I have to be honest with you. No one seems to agree with your story. In fact, the two men who were with you on this expedition . . ." She glanced down at her clipboard. "Bruno Buono and Charles Rohan, both say it didn't happen at all the way you say it did. In effect they say you're lying."

Monk shot her a pitying little smile. "The werewolves told them to say that."

"Really?"

"Yes. Those two men were threatened by the werewolves and they fear for their lives."

Ms. Delfin glanced into the camera, her face twisted into an expression that looked as if she were asking for help.

"If I am lying, then why is it that on the days I had the female wolf in custody, no one saw the ranger's daughter, Tora Brock."

The reporter looked even more pained.

"Ah, we were told you might ask that question," she said. "A check of the Redstone Secondary School attendance records showed that Tora Brock was actually in school every day during the week in question.

"What?" Monk was stunned.

"We checked," she said. "We knew you were going to bring up that point so we checked it out." She pulled a piece of paper, a copy of Tora's attendance record, from the bottom of her clipboard.

"It's wrong," Monk said. "They must have changed it. They had to."

"You mean the werewolves broke into the school?"

"No, they hacked into the school's computer. It's the only explanation."

Ms. Delfin slumped back in her seat. The interview was over and, along with it, quite possibly her career.

"Either that or it's a conspiracy," Monk raved on. "The school changed her record to cover up her absence. Wait a minute . . . yes, the whole town is probably in on it . . . hiding all proof of the werewolves' dual existence behind a veil of human technology and information."

Arlessa Delfin silently looked into the camera and motioned a flat hand, palm down, across the front of her throat in a gesture that was known the world over to mean *Cut!*

Monk, unaware that the cameras had stopped rolling – or not caring that they had – continued to babble on, and on, and on.

"Of course. How stupid of me. It's the only way they could survive and thrive among humans . . ."

•–•

It was almost sundown by the time Arlessa Delfin and her crew arrived at the Brock home for her interview with Ranger Brock.

"I'm sorry I'm so late," she said. "We interviewed Doctor Monk this afternoon and he just wouldn't stop talking."

Ranger Brock smiled. "That's all right, I have nothing planned for this evening."

Phyllis stepped into the room. "Would you and your people like some coffee?"

"Yes, actually," she answered. "We would."

The crew set up their equipment in the family room, and on the insistence of the cameraman, Ranger Brock got a fire going in the fireplace for a bit of background lighting.

Noble, Argus, Tora, and Harlan watched the crew transform the family room into a mini television studio, and all of them got a laugh out of watching Ranger Brock squirm uncomfortably as he was made up by a young woman dressed in a pair of faded jeans and white t-shirt that had the words *Be Very Afraid!* emblazoned across her chest.

But for all their interest in the goings-on, the pack stayed out of the spotlight, content to watch from the sidelines and avoid any direct questions about their identity.

"So, I guess Doctor Monk had a lot to say about what happened to him up here in our neck of the woods," Ranger Brock said when he was finally in his chair and sitting across a coffee table from the reporter.

"I'd rather talk to you about it on camera, but yes, he had *a lot* to say." The reporter paused a moment, then shook her head. "Can you believe he's blaming just about everything that happened on a bunch of teenage werewolves?" It was obvious from the woman's tone of voice that she didn't believe a word of what the doctor had to say.

Noble looked at Argus and smiled, then gave him a gentle jab with his elbow in a gesture that said, "I told you so."

"I've heard that," said Ranger Brock. "It's sad that such a brilliant man of science has to spend so much of his energy chasing myths and treating them as if they were fact."

"He does seem a bit crazy," she said, looking cautiously around her. "But you didn't hear me say that."

"Say what?" asked Ranger Brock.

"Exactly," she said with a laugh.

Later on, with the cameras rolling, Arlessa Delfin asked Ranger Brock one last question. "Perhaps you can comment on Doctor Monk's vow of returning to Redstone to bring the world proof of his claim of werewolves living in these woods."

"I wasn't aware he was planning on coming back, but if he does, we'll just have to make sure he gets a *proper* reception."

"Does that mean the werewolves will be out in force to welcome him to town?"

Ranger Brock let his head fall to one side and smiled. "We don't have any werewolves in the woods surrounding Redstone, but if he gives us enough warning, I'll make sure the local vampire brigade is ready to greet him when he arrives."

Arlessa Delfin tried to hold back her laugh, but it burst from her lips like a witch's cackle. After spending most of the day listening to Doctor Monk rant and rave, members of the crew laughed as well.

"Cut!" Ms. Delfin said, when she regained her breath. "Oh, that's perfect . . . the vampire brigade."

In the kitchen, Noble rose to his feet and gave each of his siblings a high five.

Obviously no one was ever going to believe anything Doctor Monk had to say about anything. And maybe, just maybe, the wolf pack could live their lives in peace like normal teenagers trying to grow up in the tough, cruel world of human beings.

For a little while, at least.

Acknowledgments

I am indebted to several people who helped me usher this book into the light of day. Much thanks go to the wonderful staff at Tundra Books, especially Tamara Sztainbok and Kathy Lowinger; Dr. Dan Crevier at the Brampton Veterinary Hospital; my agent, Joshua Bilmes; teenage beta tester Mikyla Graham; fellow author Michael Rowe; and of course my wife, Roberta van Belkom, without whose love and support this book and all my other books would never have been possible.